The Hardy Boys
in
The Mystery of the Melted Coins

D1332114

This Armada book belongs to:

_____

_____

_____

Other Armada Adventure Stories by Franklin W. Dixon

The Hardy Boys Mystery Stories

The Mystery of the Melted Coins

Franklin W. Dixon

Armada

First published in the U.K. in 1972 by
William Collins Sons & Co. Ltd., London and Glasgow.
First published in Armada in 1974 by
Fontana Paperbacks,
14 St. James's Place, London, SW1A 1PS.

This impression 1980.

Printed in Great Britain by
Love & Malcomson Ltd., Brighton Road,
Redhill, Surrey

CONTENTS

"Ho-Ho, so you're afraid now?" laughed Black-beard sardonically

·1·

Curse of the Caribbees

"THERE's one thing I will say for Mexican history," said Frank Hardy as he put aside the book he had been reading, "it isn't dull."

His brother Joe, working at a crossword puzzle, glanced up and grinned.

"I read that book. Very exciting. Especially those chapters about the bandits."

"They were daring all right," agreed Frank. "Those fellows must have given the government a lot of trouble."

"No doubt about that. And a Mexican bandit must have seemed mighty romantic, too. But——"

The ringing of the hall telephone interrupted Joe.

"I'll answer it," said Frank. He went into the hall and took up the receiver.

"Is Fenton Hardy there?" asked a gruff voice.

"I'm sorry. He's out just now. Any message?"

"This is Police Chief Collig speaking. Is that you, Frank?"

The boy brightened. This sounded promising. Although a telephone call from the police was nothing unusual in the Hardy home, since Mr Hardy was a private detective of international fame, the boys were sometimes called upon to lend a hand in their father's absence.

"Anything Joe and I can do, Chief?"

"Well, I'll tell you," said Collig. "I've just had a message to go over to the City Hospital. The ambulance brought in a man who was found unconscious on the street."

"Why did you want Dad?" asked Frank, puzzled.

"The fellow muttered your father's name several times, so I thought he might be a friend."

"What's the man's name?"

"Don't know," returned the chief. "No identification of any kind. I hoped your Dad would recognize him."

"Suppose Joe and I go over to the hospital and have a look at the patient."

"Wait for me," said Collig. "I'll pick you up."

Frank hurried to the living-room, explaining to Joe what had happened. "Come on," he said excitedly to his brother. "This may turn out to be a false alarm; on the other hand, it may be interesting."

The boys were outside waiting when Chief Collig's official car swung round the corner and pulled up at the kerb. They climbed in. The big man, burly and gruff, grunted a word of greeting.

"Nothing much to this business, most likely," he said. "The man will probably wake up and tell us he's John Smith from some place we never heard of. But if he *shouldn't* wake up, it might be difficult to find his relatives."

"How did he get hurt, Chief?" asked Frank. "Car accident?"

Collig shook his head. "Superintendent at the hospital says it looks as if he was beaten and robbed."

When they reached the hospital, they were whisked to the fourth floor in a lift. A nurse met them in the corridor and beckoned the group to a small ward, where a young doctor was standing by a bed.

The individual they had come to see was dark complexioned—a good-looking, black-haired man of about thirty. His eyes were closed. His head was bandaged. Frank and Joe scrutinized the unconscious patient.

"Recognize him?" asked Chief Collig.

The boys shook their heads. "Sorry, Chief. We've never seen him before," they replied.

The doctor said, "I think he's Spanish."

"Looks like a foreigner all right," agreed the chief. "But what makes you think he's Spanish?"

"He talked a little," replied the young doctor. "Just babbling, of course. Sometimes in English with a Spanish accent, and sometimes in Spanish."

"What did he talk about?"

The doctor shrugged. "All I could make out—that is, all that made sense—were the words 'Hardy' and 'Elm'. That's why I thought Fenton Hardy might know about him."

"We're Mr Hardy's sons," explained Frank. "We live on the corner of High Street and Elm Street, so perhaps Dad does know this man. You're sure he had nothing in his pockets that might identify him?"

"His pockets were cleaned out," declared the doctor. "He'd been badly beaten and probably robbed."

"Guess there's nothing more we can do here," said Chief Collig. "I've got my men searching the area where he was found. They may run across something."

"We'll ask Dad to come over and look at him as soon as he gets home," Joe promised.

The boys turned to leave. As they did so, the patient in the bed stirred. His lips moved. They heard a hoarse whisper.

At first the whisper was unintelligible. Then, clearly, the stranger muttered:

"*The Curse of the Caribbees.*"

"I wonder what it means?" Joe said wonderingly.

"He said that once before. Just after he was brought in," the doctor explained.

The injured man did not speak again, although his head stirred restlessly. Soon the police officer and the boys left the room.

"Ask your dad to run over and have a look at the man as soon as he comes home," said the chief as he drove the boys back to Elm Street. "If we can discover his name, we'll have something to work on."

Both Frank and Joe were thoughtful when they climbed out of the car and went up the steps of their house.

"*The Curse of the Caribbees,*" mused Frank. "Seems to me that this case is something more than a mere back street robbery."

They had little time to discuss the affair of the mysterious hospital patient, however, for their mother met them at the door with a telegram.

"I've been looking all over for you," she said. "Look! This just came. It was delayed."

Joe read the message aloud.

"'Arriving four o'clock train. Have boys meet me at station.'"

"Aunt Gertrude!" yelped Frank. "And here it is ten minutes past four."

The message was indeed from their Aunt Gertrude, a hot-tempered and dictatorial lady who had a habit of dropping in at Bayport unexpectedly for long visits with her brother's family. It would take plenty of explaining if she found no one to welcome her.

"Oh, gosh, I hope the train is late!" said Frank, going out of the door.

"Hurry!" urged Mrs Hardy. "You know what Aunt

Gertrude is like when things don't work out as she plans them."

"You're telling us!" laughed Joe as he raced down the steps after his brother.

Mr Hardy had taken his car, and since the boys' own car was laid up, they had to go down town by bus. But their hopes that the train might be late were doomed to disappointment.

When they hurried into the waiting-room, the first person they saw was Aunt Gertrude. She was sitting grimly on a bench, surrounded by luggage, beating an impatient tattoo on the floor with her umbrella.

She was tall, a somewhat portly woman of uncertain years, with an eye that missed nothing. But behind her forbidding manner, the boys knew there was a warm heart, a good deal of affection, and even a certain amount of quiet humour.

"Well!" barked the lady as her nephews approached sheepishly. She brandished the umbrella, pointing it at the waiting-room clock. "Does that look like four o'clock?"

"We're awfully sorry, Aunty," said Joe meekly, "but the fact is——"

"The fact is I took the trouble to send a telegram asking you to meet me at four o'clock, and here it is past four-thirty. The fact is, I've been left sitting here in this horrible waiting-room wondering what to do with myself.

"And the fact is," continued Aunt Gertrude, bringing the umbrella down on the floor with an emphatic whack that made the boys jump, "the fact is, I've been robbed!

Chet's Buried Treasure

"ROBBED?" exclaimed Frank

"You heard me. That's what I said. Robbed. It's an outrage. I'm going to the police!"

One thought quickly flashed through the minds of Frank and Joe. Was the person who had robbed their aunt the same one who had attacked the victim in the hospital?

The boys though young, had a good bit of training in detective work under the guidance of their famous father. For years Fenton Hardy had been in the service of the New York City Police Department before establishing his own practice as a private detective in Bayport.

Here Frank and Joe had spent their boyhood. Frank, dark-haired and dark-eyed, was a year older than his blond brother.

Their ambition was to become private detectives, and this ambition was backed up by ability. Success in their first case led to other cases, and at the present moment they wondered if Aunt Gertrude's robbery story would prove to be another case for them.

"What did you lose?" Frank asked her.

"I didn't lose anything. On the train I changed a five-dollar bill when I bought some fruit."

"Did he short-change you?" Joe asked.

"He gave me my exact change. I counted it. But now, now," Aunt Gertrude's voice was shrill with indignation,

"I find that some of the money isn't any good."

"Counterfeit?" gulped Joe incredulously.

The idea that anyone could outwit his aunt in any money transaction was so fantastic that he could not believe it.

"Bogus! Every single coin of it. Counterfeit money." Aunt Gertrude dug into her huge bag and fished out several coins. "Look at them! I can't imagine how I let myself be fooled like that."

To the boys, the coins looked authentic. If they were counterfeits, they certainly were very cleverly made.

"I'm going to report this to the police!" declared Aunt Gertrude firmly. "Nobody can swindle me of any money and get away with it."

At that moment an old man with dark glasses, who had been standing nearby evidently waiting for an outgoing train, shuffled forward.

"Did I hear you say you had some counterfeit money, lady?" he inquired in a cracked voice.

"And what if I did?" demanded the woman, bristling.

The stranger was not at all taken aback by Aunt Gertrude's hostile attitude, however.

"I'd like to buy 'em," he said. "I'm a coin collector. Some bogus money would be a novelty." He suggested a price.

Aunt Gertrude snorted with indignation. She glared at the old man.

"Think I don't know it's against the law to pass counterfeit money?" she barked. "I could get about five years in prison for selling a bad coin."

"Oh, lady," continued the old man in a wheedling voice, "I wouldn't tell anyone. Come on."

"I'll neither sell you one nor give you one," snapped Aunt Gertrude tartly. "I shall turn them over to my brother Fenton Hardy. He's a detective and he'll go after the men who made them."

The old man blinked through his spectacles and turned away hastily. He picked up his case and shuffled out of the waiting-room.

"Come on!" said Aunt Gertrude to her nephews. "Let's get out of here. Carry my cases. Call a taxi."

"How did you discover that the coins were counterfeit, Aunt Gertrude?" asked Joe curiously, when they were seated in the cab.

"I've handled enough of them in my time to know," she retorted mysteriously.

The Hardy boys were astonished. That any past chapter of their aunt's life could have involved her with counterfeit money seemed highly unlikely. The boys wondered if she had some secret. She did not explain further, but changed the subject abruptly. Soon the taxi arrived in front of the Hardy house.

There was always great excitement and confusion whenever Aunt Gertrude made her entrance. This time was no exception. She permitted herself to be kissed by Mrs Hardy, and then began firing out instructions.

"Take my things upstairs. . . . You, Joe, what did you do with my handbag? . . . Laura, where is Fenton? That man is never at home when I arrive."

Luckily, Fenton Hardy walked in the front door at that moment. He kissed his sister, and explained that he had returned home just a few moments after Frank and Joe set out to meet her at the station.

"Then why didn't you stay at home? Don't tell me you went down to the station too."

"No," laughed the detective. "The boys had left a message asking me to go over to the City Hospital, so I thought I could get there and back before you came."

"Did you see the mystery man?" asked Frank.

"Is he one of your clients, Dad?" Joe inquired excitedly.

Fenton Hardy shook his head. "Never saw him before. He's a total stranger to me."

"Then why did he mutter the words 'Hardy' and 'Elm'? " asked Frank, mystified.

"He may have been on his way here to consult me. We'll have to wait until he's regained consciousness before we can find out."

The case was explained briefly to the women, then Joe said, "Aunt Gertrude has a mystery of her own. She's an expert on counterfeit coins, and has some to show you," he said impishly.

His relative gave the boy a withering look. Nevertheless, she took a coin from her purse and handed it to her brother. After the detective had examined it closely, he looked at his sister admiringly.

"You're right, Gertrude," he said. "And most of the tests for counterfeits would fail on this coin, it's so cleverly done."

"You mean biting the money to see if it's soft, or dropping it to hear its ring " asked Frank.

"Exactly," replied his father. "Even the weight wouldn't be noticed by most people. This piece does not contain its value in silver, I'm sure. Probably it's made of some cheap metal with a thin coating of silver over it. I believe I'll run down to Washington to report this."

Aunt Gertrude gave her brother the rest of the coins, and then hurried upstairs.

"I'm going to get a little rest," she announced from the landing. "Frank and Joe, don't make any noise"

At that moment the doorbell rang. Before anyone

could answer the ring, in walked a chubby, red-cheeked youth who appeared to be bursting out of his clothes at every seam. He was munching a banana.

"Hi, Mrs Hardy. Hi, Aunt Gertrude. Afternoon, Mr Hardy," he greeted. Then, beckoning mysteriously to Frank and Joe, he disappeared into the kitchen. "Come out here, fellows. I have something exciting to tell you," he called.

Chet Morton's appearances were often made in this casual and unexpected manner. He was a close friend of the Hardy boys and lived in a rambling old farmhouse on the outskirts of the city. When the brothers followed him to the kitchen, they found him stuffing the last of the banana into his mouth and reaching into a biscuit jar on the table.

"Do you know," said Chet placidly, "I've never been so excited in all my life."

Frank and Joe had rarely seen Chet Morton excited about anything.

"What happened? Rich uncle die and leave you a pie factory?" laughed Joe.

"This is no laughing matter." Chet bit into a biscuit and winked mysteriously. "This is big stuff, I'm telling you." Then he lowered his voice and said in a loud whisper, "How would you two like to share in a buried treasure?"

Frank and Joe stared at him.

"Are you kidding?" asked Frank.

"You heard me," repeated Chet Morton solemnly. "I said buried treasure!"

· 3 ·

The Pine Tree Shilling

CHET fished in his pocket with a mysterious air. He took out his handkerchief, which was tied in innumerable knots.

"Do you mean to tell us you've *found* a buried treasure?" exclaimed Joe.

"Part of one. And I'm giving you fellows first chance at helping me locate the rest of it."

The fat boy was diligently untying the knots. Finally he produced a coin.

"Take a look at that!" he said impressively.

Frank and Joe examined the money. It was old and tarnished, a flat piece of silver with a crude picture of a pine tree stamped on the surface. The Hardy boys could distinguish the words "In Masathusetts."

Frank turned the coin over, and read, "New England A.N. Dom., the date 1681, and the numeral XII."

"Sixteen eighty-one!" exclaimed Frank. "Why, I didn't know they made coins in this country then."

"That," declared Chet, "is a Pine Tree Shilling. The XII means twelve cents."

"You sure it isn't some old counterfeit?" asked Joe. He could not take his friend seriously.

Chet looked hurt. "I stopped in the library on my way over here and looked it up in a book. This coin is rare and valuable."

The Hardy boys regarded their chum with respect. Although they were very fond of him, he was usually a source of amusement because he was seldom serious about anything in life except food. But here was Chet in a new role.

"Where did you get it?" asked Joe eagerly.

Chet looked round to make sure no one was listening, and then whispered hoarsely:

"Digging a ditch on our farm. Found it near the brook. I'm sure there must be more of them. Why don't you two come back home with me and spend the night? Then in the morning we can really hunt for the treasure."

"We're with you!" declared Frank, and Joe nodded.

"We'll get up bright and early in the morning and dig every inch of that field. But don't tell anyone about that coin," begged the fat boy.

"Didn't you tell your folks?" asked Joe.

Chet shook his head. "I was afraid they'd laugh at me. I'm waiting until we find the treasure. Then I'll surprise them. They'll figure I'm kind of smart after all."

Chet took another handful of biscuits. Then, with a finger to his lips in token of silence, he tiptoed out of the kitchen door and trudged across the back garden.

"Wonders will never cease," said Frank, after he had gone. "Chet Morton finding buried treasure. I can't believe it."

"It's hard to believe Chet was digging a ditch in the first place," returned Joe. "That's a miracle."

The Hardy boys laughed. Chet had never been known to be fond of work. But the brothers took the buried treasure story seriously enough to make their excuses after dinner and set out for the Mortons' place.

Chet was waiting for the boys on the porch of the roomy old farmhouse. As it was still light, he suggested they go down to the brook and have a look at the place where he had found the coin.

"Let's go before Dad or Mother or Iola have a chance to ask what we're doing," the fat boy urged. "If Joe sees Iola, we'll never get down there."

Joe's face turned red. He made no secret of the fact that he thought Chet's sister a pretty nice girl. But this time he followed his friend's suggestion and set off with the others.

Chet led the way to the field. His father had asked him to dig a drainage ditch to the brook, but apparently Chet's discovery of the coin had occurred at the first stage of the digging, for the ditch was neither deep nor long. Several spades and shovels lay about.

"Right here is where I found the money," said Chet, indicating with his toe a place near the end of the ditch.

Joe grabbed a spade. "Well, what are we waiting for?" he said. "Might as well go after the rest of the treasure now."

"That's what I say!" agreed the fat boy, seizing a shovel.

Frank also picked up a shovel, and in a few moments all three boys were working diligently. Chet, however, soon developed a stitch in his side, or so he said.

"Guess I'd better sit down for a minute. The pain'll pass off in a little while. But the doctor always warned me against violent exercise after eating."

Frank and Joe hardly noticed him. They were too busy digging—each with his eye peeled for the glint of a coin.

But after half an hour, Frank observed that Chet was still amiably inspecting their labours, though giving no indication of actually resuming work himself. He straightened up and rubbed his aching back.

"I've got an idea we're being conned," Frank said quietly to Joe. "Chet had a job to do, digging this ditch. And now we're doing it for him."

"I thought we were digging for coins," said Joe, surprised.

"That's what we both thought."

Chet, sprawled leisurely beneath a nearby tree, called out, "What's the matter—getting tired already?"

"Seems to me *you* tired pretty quickly," grinned Frank.

"You forget, I've been digging all afternoon. And besides, I've got a stitch in my side. I'll take over in a minute. No coins yet, huh?"

The Hardys resumed their digging. The more Frank thought about it, the more he was convinced that the fat boy had invented the whole story.

"I think we'd better quit," he whispered to Joe. "If we fall for this, Chet will think it's a great joke. He'll tell the story all over Bayport."

"That's what I'm thinking. Let him dig his own ditch."

"One more shovelful and I'm through."

Frank thrust the spade into the ground, and turned the earth over. Then he uttered a cry of surprise. Something struck against the edge of the spade with a dull *clink* and tumbled off to one side.

"Found something?" asked Joe.

Frank dropped the spade and picked up the object he had unearthed. It was round and metallic, covered with grime. When he brushed it off, he saw that it was a coin.

"Don't tell me you've found one!" yelped Chet, scrambling up from his resting place and displaying more energy than he had shown all evening.

He and Joe crowded round Frank as he examined the coin in the twilight. He could discern a ship on one side, and on the back of the blackened piece a figure that looked like a pig.

"Let me see it. Let me see it," babbled Chet excitedly. "Jeepers, it *is* another. I was right. There's probably a fortune buried here somewhere if we can only find it. Let's keep digging."

Frank eyed him suspiciously.

"Let *who* keep digging?"

"Why—all of us, of course."

"Haven't noticed you doing much digging tonight. Are you sure this coin isn't just bait, like the other one?"

"What do you mean?" asked Chet blankly.

"I wouldn't put it past you, Chet Morton, to plant a couple of old coins round here just to promote this ditch-digging job. I'll bet I could dig here for a month before I'd find another. But your ditch would be finished."

"On my word of honour as a gentleman," cried the stout youth fervently, "I didn't have a thing to do with putting either of those coins there! For all I know, they might have been buried in this field a hundred years ago. And I'm sure there must be more of them.

"Gee whiz," he continued, shaking his head sadly, "it sure shakes my faith in human nature. To think that my very best friends believe I'd do a thing like that. Although," he added thoughtfully, "it *would* be a smart way to get a ditch dug, come to think of it."

"It's too late to work any more tonight," Joe said. "Let's go up to the house."

"You'll help me again in the morning?" asked Chet anxiously. "Don't walk out on me now, fellows. I'll dig just the same as you. Because now I *do* believe there's a treasure. I wasn't so sure when I found just one coin," he grinned

The boys went up to the house where Mrs Morton and Iola provided a late snack, consisting of sandwiches and glasses of ice-cold milk.

"Hard work makes boys hungry," smiled Chet's mother.

"I've never noticed that it made much difference to my hard-working brother," teased Iola.

For an hour the young people talked and joked. Then the boys trooped up to bed. Tired from their exertions, they soon fell asleep.

They were up early the next morning, eager to get back to the treasure hunt. After breakfast Chet said they must hurry down to the brook.

"I never saw you so eager to work," said Iola. "What's going on?"

The boys looked a little guilty. Chet told his sister that they wanted to get the ditch dug before the sun became too hot. With that explanation, they ran off.

"We must have done a lot more digging than we thought!" exclaimed Frank, when they reached the field. "Why, the ditch is nearly finished."

"I don't remember digging any of those holes over near the tree!" declared Chet, puzzled. "And I'm sure you fellows didn't dig at that spot."

The boys stared. The spades were not where they had left them. Frank and Joe had stacked the tools neatly beside the ditch. Now they were scattered carelessly in the upturned earth.

"Someone has been here!" cried Joe. "He was digging during the night!"

"And probably found the treasure!" groaned Chet in dismay.

· 4 ·

The Intruder

THE boys looked at each other in consternation.

"Maybe he saw us working here yesterday," Chet said dolefully. "Probably stole up and listened to us talking about the treasure."

"That's possible," Frank agreed. "Are you sure you didn't tell anyone else about it?"

"I didn't tell a soul," the fat boy declared, prowling up and down the ditch.

"Maybe the fellow who was digging here last night was the man who buried the treasure in the first place," Joe suggested. "That is—if there *was* a treasure."

"The man who buried those coins has probably been dead a couple of hundred years," scoffed Chet. "I'm sure his ghost didn't come back to dig them up."

"A thief may have stolen those coins along with some others," said Joe. "Perhaps he buried them here until it was safe to come back and get them. In that case it wouldn't take him long to recover them, because he would know exactly where to hunt."

Frank shook his head doubtfully. "In that case, why did he dig an extra three feet of ditch? If he knew exactly where to go, he would have dug one hole, scooped up the treasure, and cleared out."

Chet scratched his head with a worried air. "I don't know what to make of it," he sighed. "Gee whiz—just when I thought I had a fortune in my grasp!"

"Maybe the thief didn't find it," Frank said hopefully. "He might have been confused by all the digging that's been done. Perhaps that's why he went to work on the ditch and then dug all those other holes."

Chet brightened up at this possibility. "Do you think so? Then let's start work again."

"All right," agreed Joe. "If we don't find anything, we can set up camp nearby and watch the place tonight. If the person who was here didn't find the treasure, he'll probably be back."

Chet rubbed his hands in glee. "In that case, we can let him do all the digging until he finds it. Then we'll jump out and collar the treasure. We can save ourselves a lot of trouble."

"I'd rather find the money myself," said Frank energetically.

"What money?" called out a girl's voice.

The boys turned in surprise. Iola Morton and her chum Callie Shaw were standing only a few yards away. In the soft grass they had approached without making a sound.

"What's all this about money?" Callie wanted to know. "I thought you were supposed to be digging a ditch. Looks to me as if you've been trying to find a buried treasure."

"I—I—we were just talking about money," muttered Chet. He glared at his sister. "What brings you down here anyhow?"

"We have a perfectly good reason for coming." said Iola. "There was a phone message for Frank and Joe. Your mother just called. She wants you both to come home right away."

"Anything wrong?" asked Joe quickly.

"She didn't say. I thought her voice sounded a little

shaky. But she just asked me to tell you to come home."

Frank handed his spade to Chet. "I guess you'll have to finish the ditch alone. Come on, Joe. Let's hurry."

"We'll try to come back tonight," Joe promised Chet.

"Tonight?" called Callie Shaw, puzzled. "Why on earth would you come back here at night?"

Frank decided the girls were uncomfortably close to the secret about the buried treasure.

"Maybe if Chet thinks we're not coming, he won't work," Frank smiled. "If we return, he'll be ashamed of himself unless that ditch is a good deal longer than it is now. Come on, Callie, I'll walk as far as the house with you."

Frank enjoyed Callie's company, and was sorry when he and Joe had to say goodbye. The brothers headed for home at a brisk pace.

"I hope nothing has gone wrong," Frank said. "It's unusual for Mother to call up like that. Wonder what's the matter?"

The boys made record time in reaching Elm Street. They hurried into the house, and found their mother and Aunt Gertrude in the living-room. Aunt Gertrude was peering nervously through the curtains.

"What's up?" asked Joe. "We started home as soon as we got your message."

"He's gone now," muttered their aunt strangely. "He disappeared round the corner as soon as you came in sight. You should have come in the back way."

"Who's gone? Who disappeared round the corner?" her nephew inquired.

"A strange man," said Mrs Hardy quietly. "I think he was watching this house."

Joe whistled. He turned towards the door.

"Come on, Frank. Let's find him and ask him why

he's hanging round here. What does he look like, Mother?"

"No, don't go," directed Aunt Gertrude. "We don't want to be left alone."

"Where is Dad?" asked Frank.

"He flew to Washington early this morning," Mrs Hardy told them. "He took down the counterfeit coins your Aunt Gertrude was given."

"I tell you there's more to this than meets the eye," declared the other woman grimly. "I think the man who was watching this house had something to do with those coins. Why else would he be here—except to shadow me?"

"But Aunty, how do you know he was watching *this* house?" inquired Joe.

"He pretended he *wasn't* looking at the house." snapped Aunt Gertrude. "That's exactly how I knew he *was* looking at it."

Aunt Gertrude glared at the boys triumphantly, as if defying them to dispute this logical explanation.

"He was tall, and was wearing a grey suit and a little moustache," she added, as if that settled all doubts.

Frank and Joe went to the window. "We'll keep a lookout. If he comes back, we'll see what he's up to."

But the sinister stranger did not return, and by the time lunch was ready, the boys were almost convinced that the whole affair was a false alarm.

"I guess he won't be back," said Joe, as they sat down at the table.

Just then there was a noisy disturbance in the back garden. Angry shouts and the furious barking and snarling of dogs broke the noonday peacefulness of Elm and High Streets. Aunt Gertrude leaped to her feet, sniffing battle.

Aunt Gertrude stormed into the garden. . . . .

"Now how did those dogs get into our garden?" she demanded. "I'll show them!" She stormed out through the kitchen.

Mrs Hardy and the boys followed. Two dogs were fighting viciously, and two men, presumably the owners of the animals, were arguing heatedly and loudly.

"Your dog started it!" bellowed one.

"He didn't. It was *your* dog!" shouted the other man. "Now it's up to you to stop 'em."

"Stop 'em yourself!"

By the time Aunt Gertrude waded into the argument, the racket was tremendous. She broke up the fight in five seconds flat, simply by marching right at the dogs and bawling "Get out of this garden!" in such awe-inspiring tones that they promptly fled.

But the argument between the two men was not silenced so readily. Each claimed the other's dog had started the fight. The issue became more complicated when Aunt Gertrude turned on them and blamed both of them for letting their pets get loose. It was a good fifteen minutes before the men, properly humbled and full of apologies, left the Hardy garden.

"The idea! Fighting in our back garden!" sniffed Aunt Gertrude. "Now let's finish our lunch. I declare, some people have no sense."

Joe already had entered the house. He had barely reached the kitchen, when he heard a noise from the hallway—a noise as if someone had stumbled against a chair. It was followed by the sound of hurrying footsteps.

The boy ran to the front of the house just in time to see the figure of a man disappearing through the front door. It closed sharply.

· 5 ·

The Man Who Lost his Memory

JOE raced towards the door crying, "Frank! Come quickly!"

His brother rushed into the hall just as the younger boy reached the porch.

"What's the matter?"

"Burglar!" panted Joe, hustling down the front steps.

He had caught sight of a man running along the street. The fellow turned into a drive half-way down.

The boys raced in pursuit. They reached the place just in time to see their quarry jump a hedge and disappear behind a garage, but when the boys came to the spot, the man was nowhere to be seen.

They scouted along the road, but the few minutes in which they had lost sight of the fugitive had been long enough. The man had made good his escape.

"It's no use," Frank said finally. "He is probably streets away by this time. Did you get a good look at him?"

"Not at his face," replied Joe. "But he had on a grey suit and was tall, so I guess Aunt Gertrude was right about the fellow who was watching the house."

"We'd better get back there and see if he did any damage!"

The boys hurried home to find Aunt Gertrude in a state of great agitation. She was saying that it was Mrs Hardy who was upset, however!

"Now keep calm, Laura," the woman was imploring. "You mustn't be frightened."

"I *am* calm," said Mrs Hardy, who was not half so perturbed as her relative. "You're the one who is flustered."

"Me? Flustered? Not a bit of it," said Aunt Gertrude agitatedly. "I'm as cool as a cucumber. Oh, my goodness, to think there was a burglar walking round in this house and we didn't even suspect it!"

"Did he steal anything?" asked Frank.

Mrs Hardy said she did not know. She had not had time to check. Aunt Gertrude suddenly thought of her handbag, which she had left in her room. With a cry she bounded up the stairs.

The bag was untouched—probably because Aunt Gertrude had hidden it under the mattress. But Mrs Hardy's bag, which had been lying on a living-room table, had been opened and ransacked. Fortunately, it had only held change. Nothing else was missing.

"I can't understand it," said the boys' mother. "There wasn't enough money in the house to warrant such a bold burglary."

"I have an idea," Frank said. "The man was probably the one who was watching the house this morning. The moment we went into the back garden to stop that dog fight, he slipped in by the front door."

"But how did he know we would be out of the house?" asked Mrs Hardy.

"I think that dog fight was staged on purpose," said Frank.

"You mean the other two men were accomplices of his? They started the argument with the idea of getting us out of the house, so the other fellow could get in and search the place!" exclaimed his mother.

"Doesn't it sound reasonable?"

"It seems like a lot of trouble for the sake of a few dollars," objected Mrs Hardy. "But maybe he thought there was a great deal of money here."

The Hardys returned to their interrupted lunch. All through the meal they discussed the disturbing experience. Finally Frank said:

"I believe Aunt Gertrude was right this morning. That fellow was after the counterfeit coins."

Joe blinked. "What in the world would a thief want with *counterfeit* coins? Real money—yes. But no thief would run risks to steal money he knew was no good."

"He might, if he had counterfeited them in the first place, and was afraid they would land him in jail."

Joe began to see light. "I think you've got something there. If he knew Aunt Gertrude had turned those coins over to Dad, he might have become frightened and decided to try to get them back."

"The evidence is safe in Washington by now, so he had all his trouble for nothing," said Mrs Hardy.

Just then the telephone rang and Frank answered it.

"This is the superintendent at City Hospital," said a man's voice. "About that patient you visited yesterday—the one who was beaten up. I promised your father I'd call you if there was a change in his condition."

"Is he worse?" asked Frank.

"No. In fact, he's conscious now. You can talk to him if you want to come over."

"We'll be there in ten minutes," promised Frank. Returning to the dining-room, he said, "Come along, Joe. Our mystery man has regained consciousness."

When the boys reached the hospital, they found the patient conscious and sufficiently recovered to talk But they were disappointed when they learned that the man was unable to give them the slightest clue to his identity.

"Amnesia," whispered the nurse as they stood at the bedside. "The poor man has lost his memory."

The patient looked at them blankly. "Who are you?" he asked in a weak voice with a decided Spanish accent. "I have not seen you boys before, have I?"

"When you were brought in here," said Frank, "you said something about Hardy and Elm. Well, our name is Hardy and we live on the corner of Elm and High Streets. The police thought you might be a friend of ours. We came over to see you yesterday, but we weren't of much help because we didn't know you."

"Hardy? Elm Street?" repeated the man, puzzled. He shook his head. "It means nothing to me. I am sorry."

"Can't you remember where you were going when you were injured? Were you on your way to our house?"

"I am sorry. I do not know."

"What is your name?"

The man shook his head again. "I am not able to remember anything," he muttered.

The nurse spoke up. "It's no use," she said. "His memory may come back after a while, but the doctor says it's a straight case of amnesia. He can't tell you anything."

She left the room. Frank leaned towards the bed, and looked straight at the stranger.

"Perhaps this will help you," he spoke softly to the patient. "There were a few other words you said yesterday. You muttered something about the *Curse of the Caribbees*. Does that mean anything to you?"

The man's eyes flashed. An indescribable expression of fear crossed his face.

· 6 ·

Mystery at Morton Farm

FRANK was sure the words had hit home.

"*The Curse of the Caribbees?*" asked the man sharply. Then his face became expressionless again, and his eyes lost their momentary gleam of panic. "Never have I heard of it."

The boys decided there was nothing to be gained by questioning the mysterious patient any further. But when the boys reached the street, Joe asked his brother, "Do you think he's faking?"

"That remark about the *Curse of the Caribbees* seemed to upset him. If he really has amnesia, it shouldn't have bothered him at all. I'll bet he's afraid of someone."

"He looked scared to me. Maybe that expression means so much to him that it's one of the few things he hasn't forgotten."

"I think we ought to tell Chief Collig about this."

Down at Bayport police headquarters they told the chief their story. He frowned.

"The fellow *might* be faking," Collig admitted, "although the doctor at the hospital seemed pretty sure the amnesia was genuine. But that doesn't mean he isn't a crook. I'd better have a guard stationed near his room."

"And if he isn't a crook, he may need protection," suggested Joe. "The fellows who beat him up may try the same stunt again."

"He's a mystery man, sure enough," declared the chief. "He'll need watching."

He thanked the boys for their information. The Hardys left and headed for home.

A surprise awaited the brothers when they reached their house. Fenton Hardy was home. He was in the living-room, listening to Mrs Hardy's account of the burglary.

"What did the thief take?" asked the detective, frowning.

"Apparently nothing but a little money," replied Mrs Hardy. "I still can't understand why he came here."

The boys' father suddenly rose from his chair.

"I believe I know what the fellow was after," he said, "and maybe he got it."

The detective went to his study. Taking a small key from his pocket, he opened a drawer in his desk. Then he pressed a concealed spring. The drawer had a concealed back which slid away, revealing a secret hiding place behind it. He looked inside, then closed the desk.

"The other counterfeit coins are still here," Mr Hardy smiled, returning to the living-room.

"You didn't take them all with you?" asked Joe.

"Suppose I had been held up, or lost the fake money? All my evidence would have been gone," the detective chuckled. "I didn't think any thief could find this hiding place. But I felt reasonably sure that's what the intruder was looking for just the same.

"They are very good imitations," he continued. "The men down in Washington hadn't seen any quite like these before. They said the coins are about the best fakes they have come across. They sent their thanks to you, Gertrude, and wondered how you detected the counterfeits so easily."

His sister sniffed, tossed her head, and said, "Hmph. A body would think I didn't have any brains at all."

She bustled out of the room, but her nephews thought she smiled mysteriously as she went upstairs. Did their aunt have some secret she was keeping to herself?

"Sometime, boys," remarked Mr Hardy, "I want you to see the wonderful collection of coins that are on display in Washington."

"I wish I knew more about old money right now," said Frank, thinking of Chet's treasure. "When were the first pieces made, Dad?"

"The experts say the first ones appeared in Asia Minor about 750 B.C. The Chinese, too, had metal money long ago. They were clever at testing it to keep from being cheated. They could tell if a coin was genuine merely by holding it between the thumb and first finger."

"Speaking of the Chinese," remarked Joe, "we have someone here in Bayport who is pretty clever on that subject. Old Wu Sing."

"That's right," agreed his father. "He has a good collection of old money."

"Let's look at it on our way back to Chet's," suggested Frank to his brother with a wink. He was thinking of Chet's coins. "It's all right to go to the Mortons now, isn't it Dad?"

"Yes. But before you go, how about doing a little work in the garden here? Grass, weeds—you know how it is."

"All right," the two sons promised, and Frank added, "We can't be detectives every minute, I suppose."

Before they went outside, the boys told their father of the latest developments in the case of the amnesia patient whom Frank had nicknamed "Mr Spanish".

Mr Hardy said he would take a trip over to the hospital to talk to the strange man.

"Oh, I almost forgot to tell you," he smiled. "The official I saw in Washington asked me to tell you boys to keep your eyes open. Maybe you can land some counterfeiters!"

"You bet we will," said Frank, and Joe nodded. "Nothing would suit us better."

Weeds in the garden were more numerous than the boys had suspected, and it was six o'clock before their job was done. As soon as dinner was over, they set out for the Mortons without stopping at Wu Sing's to see his collection. It was nearly dark when they reached the farmhouse. Iola met them at the door.

"Can you imagine it!" she exclaimed. "Chet loves that old ditch so much he's actually sleeping down there. We can't understand it. He set up a tent under the trees this evening. He's expecting you. I suppose you'll sleep there too!"

"We'll go right down."

"Something strange has happened to that boy," said Iola, mystified. "Usually he hates work so much. . . ."

The Hardy boys gave no explanation. In a few minutes they said good night to Iola and went down across the fields towards the brook. There was no light in evidence, but in the moonlight they could see the grey shape of a tent which had been set up under the trees.

"Chet must have gone to bed early," Frank remarked quietly.

"He probably dug a whole square yard of ditch today and is exhausted," laughed Joe. "Let's steal up and surprise him."

They moved forward silently through the soft grass. As they came closer to the brook, they heard a surprising sound. It was a sharp ring of metal, as if a spade had clattered against a rock.

"Don't tell me that Chet is still working!" whispered Joe incredulously. "I can't believe it!"

"Listen!"

The boys halted. They could hear unmistakable sounds of digging. Then, as they strained their eyes, they could distinguish a figure near the ditch. It crouched, straightened up, then crouched again.

"What do you know about that!" gasped Joe. "Iola was right. There *is* something the matter with Chet. He's working at that ditch even in the dark!"

"Hey, Chet!" shouted Frank.

The Hardys hurried across the meadow. A slight rise in the ground hid the ditch from view for a moment. When the boys came over the top and ran down the slope, they could no longer see anyone around.

"Funny he didn't answer," remarked Joe.

"Maybe he didn't hear us. It's strange he isn't using a light."

When the brothers reached the spot a moment later, it was deserted. A spade lay beside the freshly dug earth.

"Chet!" called out Frank again.

There was no answer.

The boys turned towards the tent, which was pitched a few yards away. Frank whipped a torch from his pocket as he thrust aside the flap and went in.

"Come on, Chet," he laughed. "We saw you working. No denying it. You——"

The beam of light revealed a figure sprawled on the ground. Frank leaped forward.

Chet Morton lay there—unconscious!

Wu Sing

"GET some water, Joe. Quick!"

Joe snatched up a small pail that was lying with Chet's camp equipment, and ran towards the brook while Frank set about trying to revive their chum.

When Joe dashed in with the pail of water, they splashed it in Chet's face and his eyes flew open. He sat up, spluttering.

"What hit me?" he moaned, rubbing the back of his head.

"That's what Frank and I would like to know. We thought we heard you digging when we came across the field. But it must have been someone else. When we came in, we found you sprawled here—out cold."

"Somebody whammed me over the head," grunted Chet. He rubbed the base of his skull. "Feel that lump? That guy really socked me."

"Who socked you?"

Groggy, Chet shook his head. "I wish I knew. I was tired out from digging and I thought you fellows weren't coming, so I decided to rest for a minute. I must have fallen asleep. When I woke up, I heard someone coming into the tent. I thought it was you and Joe. So I sat up and said, 'Well, it's about time you showed up,' and just then the roof seemed to fall in."

"Maybe the fellow isn't far away," Joe said excitedly. "I'm going to hunt for him!"

"Be careful!" warned Chet. "He's likely to knock your brains out. Better let him go."

Joe paid no heed. He ran out past the ditch and headed towards the fence. In the moonlight he looked up and down a nearby lane and across the fields. There was no sign of movement. The mysterious stranger had lost no time in making himself scarce. In disgust Joe returned to the others.

"No luck," he reported. "Let's look round and see what he was up to."

They found a deep, fresh hole at the edge of the ditch.

"I'm sure someone buried loot here and came back for it," decided Frank. "The question is—was he successful or wasn't he?"

"Judging by the size of that hole I think he knew exactly where to dig this time," Joe remarked. "It must have been mighty important to him, too, to warrant slugging Chet."

"He wasn't fooling," observed the fat boy ruefully. "He really meant to put me to sleep."

"I wonder if the pine tree coin and the other one we found were part of the loot the man was looking for," said Frank slowly. "Or were they just silver pieces dropped here long ago by some farmer or traveller?"

"One thing seems sure," Joe remarked after they had discussed it all. "If the crook was frightened away before he found what he was hunting for, he'll probably be back. I think we ought to take turns standing guard here for the rest of the night."

The others agreed this was a sound idea.

"If he should return, the one on guard can warn the other two and we'll all tackle him," said Frank. "I'll take the first watch if you like. It's nearly eleven o'clock now. I'll keep a look out until one."

"Then wake me and I'll take over until three o'clock," offered Joe. "Chet can stand guard until five."

"Suits me," agreed the fat boy. "I'm glad I don't have first watch. I want sleep right now, and plenty of it."

Chet and Joe returned to the tent, while Frank took up his vigil. By one o'clock, when Joe took over, there had been no sign of the stranger's return; nor had anything occurred to disturb his watch by the time Chet was aroused. At sunrise he crept back into the tent.

"Just a waste of time," he muttered. "That guy probably got my treasure and now I'll never find it, worse luck."

Early in the morning, before they went up to the farmhouse for breakfast, the boys explored the ground round the ditch. In the freshly-turned earth they found a man's footprints leading towards the fence by the lane. They followed the tracks farther and were able to make them out for several hundred yards. They vanished at the main road. Tyre marks told the rest of the story.

"The man had a car parked here. After we disturbed his digging, he climbed the fence, ran this far, and then drove off," Frank explained.

"I'm going to take an impression of these footprints," declared Frank, "and stop at police headquarters with them. Maybe Chief Collig will recognize them."

"Guess I'll stay here," said Joe. "Chet and I will work some more. You go on home. We'll let you know if anything turns up."

"I think I'll run in and see Wu Sing while I'm in town," said Frank. "Let me have the two coins, Chet. He may be able to give us some help with this mystery."

Chet handed over the silver pieces.

"Don't say where they were found," he warned. "If

that news should get out, everyone in the city will be up here digging like mad."

"It would be a good story to circulate, if you should want to get a garden dug in a hurry," grinned Joe.

After breakfast, Frank returned to Bayport. At police headquarters he was disappointed. There was no record of any footprints like those which the boy showed the chief.

"Working on another case?" asked the officer, smiling.

"Sort of," replied Frank, and hurried away.

He found Wu Sing, a gentle, elderly Chinese merchant, in an office at the rear of his shop. The old man beamed with pleasure when the boy came in.

"You come to see Wu Sing? This is great pleasure," he said, bowing. "You come sit down, please."

"Wu Sing, you know a good deal about coins," said Frank. "That's why I've called to see you."

The Chinese shrugged deprecatingly. "There is much to know about them," he said. "I know a little. Very little. But if I can help you, I will be glad."

Frank took the two silver pieces from his pocket and handed them over.

"Do you think these are genuine?" he asked.

Wu Sing put the coins in his palm and examined them carefully. Then he took them over to the window and looked at them in the sunlight.

"Yes," he said quietly. "Very rare. Early American Pine Tree Shilling, this one. The other—I shall have to look."

He pulled a catalogue from a drawer and thumbed through it.

"Here is picture. Coin was made at Hog Island about 1620. It is called Hog Coin."

"Where is Hog Island?" asked Frank.

"Now we call it Bermuda. Once the wild hogs roamed the place. May I ask where you got these coins?"

"They were found in a field near Bayport," Frank explained. "I'm not sure, but there may have been more of them. We thought perhaps they had been stolen."

"If stolen," said Wu Sing, examining the pieces again, "then I think thief stole them from numismatist."

"From a coin collector?"

"No one else likely to have such rare ones as these. If someone lose collection of early American coins, then maybe these are clues of value."

"You collect coins yourself, Wu Sing?" asked the Hardy boy.

The Chinese shook his head. "I study coins but I collect only Chinese pieces. Mr Carter here in Bayport has good coin collection. Also Doctor Wakefield. Maybe if you ask them, they help you."

"That's a good idea," Frank declared. "I'll go and see Mr Carter first. He lives near here."

Wu Sing examined the coins carefully again, then returned them to the boy.

"Most interesting. Fine specimens," he said. "A story behind their discovery, no doubt?" His eyes twinkled.

"I'll tell you about it as soon as I can, Wu Sing," said Frank. "In the meantime, watch your own collection carefully. Don't let anybody steal it."

· 8 ·

The Tattooed Head

"No, my collection is safe, thank goodness," declared Phineas Carter when Frank called on him.

He was a jolly, red-faced business man who had now retired and lived quietly. When the Hardy boy showed him the two early American coins, he was tremendously interested, and offered to buy them on the spot.

"I'm sorry Mr Carter, but they're not for sale. I thought possibly they had been stolen from a private collection."

"So now you're trying to find a coin collector who has been robbed, eh? Well, I'm glad to say my pieces haven't been touched. There was a stranger around yesterday, though, who wanted to see them. Odd-looking old duck."

"An elderly man wearing dark spectacles?" asked Frank eagerly.

"Why, yes. Do you know him?"

Thinking of the old man in the railway station, the boy replied:

"Not exactly, but I did run across a person of that description who was interested in coins. You say he was looking at your collection?"

"Said he might be interested in buying something from it, but I didn't have what he was looking for," returned Mr Carter. "He told me his name was Ratchy."

Frank thanked the collector and left the house. He

was excited now and wondered if he had uncovered an important lead.

"I'll go to see Doctor Wakefield," the boy decided. "If Ratchy has been to visit him, I'll know there's something in the wind."

Doctor Wakefield, a retired professor, lived a few streets away. Stooped and grey haired, he blinked at Frank over his glasses when the youth announced the purpose of his call.

"It seems to me a number of people are interested in my little collection," he beamed. "A man came round to look at my coins only yesterday."

"Is that so?" said Frank. "Did he want to buy any?"

"That's what he said. But I didn't have anything he wanted. He was an old fellow by the name of Ratchy. You aren't buying coins, are you?"

"No. I have a couple of rare ones that were found, and I thought they might have come from a collection. I was wondering if you had lost any."

"No," smiled the professor. "I was looking at them not ten minutes ago, and I am sure that every coin is in its proper place."

"I'm glad of that, Doctor Wakefield."

After Frank had seen the display and admired it, the old man explained the fascination of coin collecting.

"The study of coins gives one a good knowledge of history, geography and the customs of people. Some of the ancient rulers used to commemorate nearly everything they did by setting it forth on a new piece of money. One old Roman Emperor had ten thousand varieties issued!"

"He must have loved himself a great deal," laughed Frank.

"Well, my collection is very insignificant," said the

professor. "I doubt that any thief would be interested in it. But if I should lose anything, I'll let you know."

Frank expressed his appreciation for the time given him, then went home. Aunt Gertrude wanted to know what was going on.

"I never saw such a family," she said. "In and out, in and out all the time," she scolded. "Your father won't be back for lunch, and your mother has gone to a club meeting. Never saw such a household for people gadding about all the time."

At noon Joe telephoned his brother and was told of Frank's recent adventure, including the story about the calls of the mysterious old man on the collectors.

"First, Mr Ratchy wants to buy a counterfeit coin," said Frank, speaking in a low voice on the upstairs telephone. "Then he visits two coin collectors, looking for something they don't have!"

"Do you think that might have been an excuse to see how valuable the collections were? He really didn't want to buy any of them?" asked Joe.

"Exactly. Well, I found out one thing. If those coins from the Morton field were stolen from a collection they probably weren't stolen in Bayport, as Mr Carter and Doctor Wakefield are the only two who own very many pieces."

Joe reported that he and Chet had unearthed nothing of value. Just then Frank heard his name called. He hung up the telephone and came downstairs. His mother, who had just returned from her meeting, was in the living-room opening her handbag. Aunt Gertrude stood nearby.

"I'm glad you're back, son," she smiled. "Will you do an errand for me?"

"Anything you like, Mother," said Frank promptly.

Then he gasped as Mrs Hardy took from her purse a large sum of money. "Looks as if you've been to the bank."

"Looks as if I should go to the bank," declared Mrs Hardy. "You know I'm treasurer of the club. Today most of the members paid their annual subscriptions and I'm simply swamped with money," she laughed.

"The sooner it's out of this house the better," declared Aunt Gertrude tartly. "It's an invitation to thieves."

"Don't worry, Gertrude, I haven't any intention of keeping it. It has to go to the bank in Mawling before closing time."

"Mawling?" exclaimed Frank in surprise. Mawling was a small village several miles from Bayport. "What's the matter with the banks here?"

"Well, the club account has always been kept there because the first treasurer lived in Mawling. After she retired, we didn't bother to transfer the account. Frank can drive over as soon as we've had lunch," decided Mrs Hardy.

The meal was eaten without any excitement, however, except that Aunt Gertrude kept getting up and going to the door every few minutes.

Despite this, she had failed to see a sinister, furtive-eyed man who had slunk across the lawn. From a vantage point among the bushes underneath a window, he had been eavesdropping ever since Mrs Hardy had entered the house. At last, with a grim smile on his face he tiptoed away and climbed into a car parked by the kerb some distance down the street.

Soon afterwards Frank left the house with the money in his pocket. When he drove out of the garage ten minutes later, the other car drew away from the kerb and started down the road in pursuit.

After leaving the outskirts of the city, Frank turned on to a road that led to the village of Mawling. In the rear-view mirror he noticed the other car some distance behind, but paid it no particular attention.

A lonely side road offered a short cut to the village. Hardly had Frank left the main road before he noticed that the other car was overtaking him. He pulled over to let it pass, but it came alongside, forcing him towards the ditch. Frank looked up in alarm.

Then he saw that the driver was masked!

A crash was imminent. The man had cut off the boy. Frank jammed on the brakes before he was forced into the ditch. At the same moment he flung open the door and jumped.

He had a pretty good idea of what the masked person was after—the money he was taking to the bank in Mawling! Like a streak of lightning the boy leaped over the ditch, but just beyond it was a fence. He had nearly cleared this, when a man lunged forward and tackled him.

The struggle was brief. Frank fought vigorously, but his assailant was bigger and stronger. During the battle, the youth tried to pull off the mask to catch a glimpse of the other's face. It moved slightly to one side, but did not come off.

In the struggle Frank did rip open the front of the fellow's shirt. The boy had a glimpse of a strange design tattooed on the man's chest—a design in the crude likeness of a Spanish woman's head.

Then something struck him violently on the skull. As he pitched forward, everything went black.

Grinning evilly, the hold-up man went through the boy's pockets, and made his escape. Frank was left lying on the ground.

The Old Man With the Dimes

GROANING, Frank opened his eyes. He sat up and rubbed his aching head. Then, suddenly remembering what had happened, he clapped his hands to his pockets. The money his mother had given him was gone!

"That's bad," he thought. "But Chet's coins are here," the boy sighed, when he discovered them a moment later. "Glad the thief missed them."

Groggily, the lad pulled himself to his feet. He examined the tyre marks in the dusty road. The masked man had turned his car around and driven back towards the highway.

Frank got into his own car and followed. At the tarmac the tell-tale marks were mixed with others, and there was no indication of the direction which the hold-up man had taken.

Without the club money, Frank realized there would be no use in going on to Mawling. Sick at heart over the loss, he returned to Bayport. When Aunt Gertrude saw him coming in the front door, she uttered a cry of amazement.

"Here already! You must have driven at a hundred miles an hour. Young man, you'll be arrested for speeding one of those days——"

"I know why he came back," smiled Mrs Hardy. Then she noticed her son's white face and stricken look. "Why, what's the matter, dear?" she asked anxiously.

"I lost the money. Hold-up man forced me off the road and stole it all."

The dejected boy trudged to the telephone and called Bayport Police Headquarters. Dully, he reported the loss.

"That's too bad, Frank," said the desk sergeant. "I'll send out a call on the police radio. Too bad you weren't able to get the fellow's licence number. How much money did you lose?"

"Quite a bit—about five hundred dollars, I think. How much was it, Mother?" Frank asked.

"Not as much as that," she said sympathetically. "In fact, I thought that was why you returned. After you left, I noticed I had made a mistake and hadn't given you the whole amount. You had only a hundred and fifty with you. The rest is here."

"Well, that's a break, anyway," said Frank, feeling better. "A hundred and fifty in notes," he told the desk sergeant.

"We'll do the best we can to get it back," promised the officer. "Tell us what you know about the fellow."

The boy told of the strange tattoo mark on the thief's chest—a crude design of a Spanish woman's head.

"That's a good clue," the sergeant praised. "Well, we'll do our best."

As Frank turned to his mother and aunt, the latter said:

"I shouldn't be surprised if the thief were the man who robbed this house yesterday. Maybe the same one who was hanging round here in the morning."

"No, this fellow was much bigger and heavier," declared Frank. He glanced at the clock. "Gosh, I must have been out cold a long time. It's too late to go to the bank now."

He was glad to get to bed early, and he fell asleep at once. After a good rest he felt quite himself again.

Soon after breakfast the next morning Joe came in. He had no news to report from the Morton farm, but he whistled when he heard of his brother's mishap.

"You'd better go with me to the bank this morning," Frank grinned. "Guess I need a bodyguard."

"I'm ready. Well, I'm glad the fellow didn't take Chet's coins. They can't be replaced."

This time, on the drive to Mawling, Frank took no short cuts. He stayed on the main road all the way.

"That was the most expensive short cut I ever took," he told Joe. "Most likely the hold-up wouldn't have happened at all if I'd kept to this road."

The boys drove into Mawling, and pulled up in front of the bank. Going inside, they found there was just one customer at the counter ahead of them—an old man.

"Wouldn't think there was so much money in all those dimes," he was chuckling, as the cashier handed him several twenty-dollar notes.

"It takes a good while to count such a lot," said the cashier. Before him, in neat paper-rolled stacks, were several hundred dimes. "I don't blame you for wanting to get rid of them."

"Paper money is easier to carry," cackled the old man. He thrust the bills nto a wallet and turned away.

There was something oddly familiar about his voice. When the Hardy boys looked at his face intently, they were sure they recognized him.

He was the man who had tried to buy the counterfeit coins from Aunt Gertrude! But he was not wearing dark glasses. Was he also the person who had visited the coin collectors?

The old fellow was too absorbed in his money to pay the boys any attention. He thrust the wallet into his pocket and shuffled towards the door.

When he had gone outside, Frank stepped up to the window. The teller was busy putting away the stacks of dimes.

"That was a job, I must say," he remarked. "I've been counting these coins here for the past quarter-hour. That man seemed to have a ton of them."

"Where did he get so many?"

"Said he had been in charge of a children's entertainment somewhere," the teller said. "I suppose it was the admission money."

"Do you know the old man's name?" asked Joe eagerly.

The teller shook his head. "Never seen him before," he replied carelessly. "Now what can I do for you chaps?"

Frank deposited the money Mrs Hardy had given him. He also wrote out a cheque from his own account in a Bayport bank for the amount that had been stolen from him and deposited that as well.

"It seems strange," Joe said, when the boys had left the bank and were driving towards home, "that every time we come across that old man, he is in some way connected with coins. I wish we had followed him."

"If we ever see him again, let's do it."

Aunt Gertrude was much relieved when the boys reached home and reported that the money had been safely banked. She said she had not drawn an easy breath since the boys had left the house.

Late that afternoon they set out on foot for the Morton farm. Chet, to their astonishment, was actually working.

"Thought I might as well do a little more digging to

fill in the time," he explained defensively. "Who knows but that other coin may turn up?" He set aside his spade and sat down on the grass. "What's new?"

"Plenty," said Frank.

He told Chet of the hold-up and of their suspicions about the strange old man.

"I *knew* I should have gone along with you, Joe, instead of staying here all day!" declared the fat boy. "You fellows have all the excitement! Say, did that hold-up man get my coins?"

"No, thank goodness," replied Frank, and handed over the Pine Tree Shilling and the Hog Coin.

He explained what Wu Sing had told him. Then the conversation turned back to the strange old man.

"Maybe that Ratchy person was the one who was digging here," suggested Chet.

"Too old," said Joe. "He couldn't have run away as fast as that fellow did the other night."

"Then maybe it was the hold-up man who was here," offered Chet.

"Could be," said Frank. "Only, if he were interested in old coins, why didn't he take yours when he had the chance?"

"Maybe he didn't find them," said Chet in defence of his own deductions.

The boys went on with their digging. In a little while Chet declared he was so hungry he could not lift a shovel, so the three boys went up to the house. Supper was not ready, but Chet found part of a pie in the fridge, and by eating it, managed to survive until Mrs Morton had the meal on the table. Again Iola wanted to know what the mystery was behind the boys' unusual interest in the ditch-digging job.

"All in good time, young lady. All in good time,"

Chet informed his sister in a lordly manner. "Just be patient and everything will be revealed to you."

"There certainly must be something behind it," smiled Mrs Morton. "I'm sure it isn't fondness for work on your part."

"I'm misjudged and not appreciated," sighed her son. "I work like a dog, digging from morning until night, and this is all the thanks I get."

That evening the boys went back to the field. They made their camp a little more comfortable, and then sat chatting under the trees until dusk fell. The boys were talking over who should stand guard first, when Joe suddenly grabbed Frank's arm and pointed in the direction of the lane.

"Someone coming," he whispered.

Then Frank saw a light—a wavering, bobbing light. It flickered out, then shone again, and moved steadily across the field. Beyond it they could see the vague shape of a shadowy figure.

"Great Scot!" squeaked Chet. "He's heading this way!"

· 10 ·

"Mr Spanish"

THE boys watched.

The man with the torch walked so quietly that his footsteps made no sound in the soft grass. When he came close to the tent, Frank murmured:

"Looking for someone?"

There was a startled gasp. The stranger swung round turning the torch full on the three figures.

"Tarnation!" he grunted. "Why didn't you speak up before this? Almost scared the daylights out of me."

The boys laughed in relief, for they recognized the voice as that of Officer Con Riley of the Bayport police.

"What on earth are you doing out here so far off your beat?" asked Joe

"Looking for you fellows," said Riley. "Chief Collig sent me to find you. Wants to see you at headquarters. I went round to your house to get you, and your aunt said I'd likely find you at the Mortons. At the house they told me you were down here."

"Chief Collig wants to see us? What for?"

"How should I know?" muttered Riley. "All I was told is he wants to see you, and quick. So you'd better come along. I've got a car."

"For a couple of guys who came out here to *help* me," complained Chet, "you two certainly can find a lot of reasons for quitting the job."

"We didn't find this one. It found us," chuckled Joe.

Down at Bayport Police Headquarters, Chief Collig was waiting for them. He called the boys into his private office.

"It's about that hold-up yesterday," he explained. "We picked up a few suspects, Frank, all with tattoos on their chests. I want you to take a look at them."

He led the boys downstairs to a room in the basement. At the far end of it was a raised platform, with a glare of electric lights overhead. Chief Collig signalled to an officer, who opened a door at one side of the platform.

Four men shuffled out in the custody of a sergeant. They blinked in the brilliance of the lights. Frank studied them and their tattoo marks carefully. Finally he turned to Chief Collig and shook his head.

"The hold-up man was not any of these four," he said. "Tattoo marks are different."

"Okay," returned the officer. "I don't have much hope. We'll keep trying." He called to the sergeant, "Turn the men loose, Stan."

The chief explained to the boys why he had sent for them in a hurry. "We couldn't hold these suspects for long, because we haven't anything on them. That's why I wanted you to look at them tonight, Frank."

"Too bad they had to be brought in here for nothing," said Joe.

"Don't waste any sympathy on that bunch," the chief laughed. "They're all bad. They've been in and out of jail several times. If none of them pulled that hold-up job, it was only because he didn't happen to think of it!"

When the boys left the police station they decided that since it was still early enough to call at City Hospital, they would inquire about the amnesia victim.

Mr Hardy had not found time to go, and the boys were curious to learn something about "Mr Spanish's" condition. At the hospital, they were told that the mysterious patient had shown considerable improvement during the day.

"He still doesn't know his own name," the ward sister said. "But apart from that he's well enough to walk out of here tomorrow."

"Mr Spanish" was sitting up in bed, obviously in much better condition than on their previous call and when the Hardys approached, he smiled pleasantly at them.

"You were here before," he said. "It is good of you to come to see me again. I wish you could help me find out who I am."

"I wish we could, 'Mr Spanish'— " began Joe.

The man's eyes went up in polite astonishment. "What is it you call me—'Mr Spanish'? "

"We had to give you some kind of a name," laughed Frank, "and because of your accent, we decided on 'Mr Spanish'. You don't know where you're from?"

The patient shook his head sadly.

"Perhaps I shall never know. It is a terrible thing, this, to recall nothing of one's past. Where I came from, how I came to be here—it is all a puzzle."

"There was one thing we said to you last time we were here that you seemed to recognize," related Joe. "You later told us it meant nothing to you. Suppose we try it again. *The Curse of the Caribbees*."

"Mr Spanish" frowned thoughtfully. This time the boys were convinced that the man was making an honest effort to remember.

"*The Curse of the Caribbees*," he repeated slowly. Finally he shook his head. "No. If it meant anything to me, I would tell you gladly. But truly it awakens nothing in my memory."

"Maybe it will later," said Frank kindly.

Just then the nurse came up and informed the boys that the visiting period was over. They promised "Mr Spanish" that they would come to see him again.

"My opinion of him has changed," Frank told the nurse after they left the room. "He doesn't seem to be a crook."

"You're right. And I'm sure I don't know what's to become of him," the woman said. "He's well enough to leave here, but where is he to go? The doctor was saying today that since he probably was on his way to see Mr Hardy when he got hurt, perhaps you might take him. We're so crowded here just now——"

When the hospital doors had closed behind the boys and they were going down the steps, Joe said:

"Well, was that a hint or wasn't it?"

"It was more than a hint," laughed Frank. "Let's see what the folks think about it."

When the boys reached home, they found Mrs Hardy and Aunt Gertrude in the living-room talking with Mr Hardy, who had returned a few minutes before.

"Just like I said," spoke up Aunt Gertrude at once, as the brothers walked in. "In and out. In and out. I thought you were staying at the Morton place tonight."

Joe explained that they had dropped in to talk over a proposition regarding the amnesia victim, and then would go back to Chet's.

" 'Mr Spanish' is getting better," said Frank. "He doesn't know his name yet, and he hasn't regained his memory, but he's well enough to leave the hospital."

"We thought it might be a good idea to invite him to come here," said Joe.

Mrs Hardy looked thoughtful. Fenton Hardy raised his eyebrows enquiringly. As for Aunt Gertrude, she promptly exploded.

"What's that? Bring a crazy man to live in this house? Nonsense! I'll take the first train out of Bayport."

"But he isn't crazy, Aunty," explained Joe. "The poor fellow has merely lost his memory."

"Practically the same thing," sniffed Aunt Gertrude. "I'd go crazy trying to remember things. Well, if that man comes to this house, you boys will have to stay here and watch him. It wouldn't be fair to your mother or me to leave us alone with a stranger."

She flounced from the room. The boys asked their father what he thought of the idea.

"I'm all for it," declared Fenton Hardy. "Quite aside from the fact that it would be a decent and generous thing to do, because the poor fellow is homeless and penniless in a strange country, I'd really like to know why 'Mr Spanish' came to Bayport. If he is with us when his memory comes back to him—as it should eventually—then we'll know what was behind it all."

Mr Hardy looked towards his wife, who smiled understandingly. "I'll be glad to have the poor man, if he'll stay with us," she said kindly.

"We'll bring him here tomorrow," spoke up Joe.

"But your Aunt Gertrude is right about you boys having to stay at home," said Mr Hardy. "No more treasure digging."

Frank and Joe jumped. "Then you know?" they gasped, looking at their father.

The detective smiled. "I *didn't* know until you boys gave yourselves away. Just plain deduction. Point one: Chet Morton doesn't like physical exercise, so why in the world would he be working day and night?

"Point two: why would his two best friends want to camp out in a field day and night and work, unless they were hunting for something pretty important, like a buried treasure?"

The boys looked admiringly at their father.

"Gosh Dad, you're wonderful!" said Joe. His face glowed.

Mrs Hardy's eyes twinkled. "Have you just found that out, son?" she asked him.

"Oh, no," replied Joe in embarrassment, "but I was thinking it wouldn't pay to try to keep a secret from Dad!"

"Surely your father hasn't guessed everything you are doing," said his mother in defence of her sons' keenness. "There is more to the mystery than you have admitted, isn't there?"

Frank and Joe looked at her gratefully.

"Even if we don't find a treasure, we think we may capture a thief one of these days," replied Frank. "A coin thief."

He told his parents what he and Joe suspected about the fellow who had knocked Chet Morton unconscious. It was Mr Hardy's turn to look surprised.

"Good work," he praised them. "I hope you catch the man. Well, you boys had better go back to the Mortons, or Chet may get into trouble. But tell him to find another pal to help him from now on. You'll be needed here."

"To watch 'Mr Spanish'?" said Frank, a questioning look in his eyes.

"Yes. I have to make a business trip. A representative of a foreign government has asked me to take a very interesting case. I suspect it may have something to do with melted coins. I'll tell you about it."

The Secret Pocket

FRANK and Joe settled themselves in chairs to hear their father's story.

"The man who asked me to handle the case for his government has been disturbed for some time over a certain situation," Mr Hardy continued. "It seems that two years ago his country shipped thousands of gold coins to the United States in payment of certain debts."

"I thought gold was always shipped in bars," said Frank.

"Usually it is, yes," replied his father. "But trouble was brewing in that country, and the officials sent off the coins for fear they would be seized. Some of the shipment was in bullion, to be sure, but a lot of it was in coin, packed in strong cases. The money was sent to the United States by boat. But a severe storm came up.

"The boat didn't sink, but it was badly damaged, and put into Barmet Bay near here for repairs. The next day the captain decided to move the gold coins ashore for safe-keeping. But when he gave the order, he found that the money had disappeared."

"All of it?" asked Joe.

"The entire shipment had vanished completely. What's more, none of the gold bars or coins have ever been found. It was thought at first that it would merely be a matter of time before there would be some clue.

But from that day to this there hasn't been a trace of any of the gold," Mr Hardy concluded.

"Maybe it was melted down and turned into United States coins," Frank suggested.

"I hardly think so. Gold money is too easy to spot, for there isn't much of it in circulation," his father replied. "But you have given me an idea. Maybe the coins were melted, but for another reason. I believe I'll follow that lead while I'm away.

"First I'll fly to New York, though, to check on a couple of points, then I'll return here before going farther. Suppose you trot along to Chet's and be home by lunchtime tomorrow. Then we'll drive over to the hospital together and get 'Mr Spanish'. "

Mr Hardy would divulge no more of his case, so the boys followed his suggestion and left the house. Frank and Joe found their fat friend sound asleep in the tent near the brook.

"Hey, what kind of guard are you?" grinned Frank, poking his friend in the ribs.

"Whassa matter?"

Chet opened his eyes a moment, then closed them and rolled over.

"Get up!" commanded Joe. "You've had a nice nap. You ought to take first watch."

"What for?" asked the stout boy, yawning.

"To catch the thief who buried some loot here," Frank reminded him.

"Oh! That's right! High time you fellows got back," his friend grumbled.

Chet arose, and disappeared outside. The Hardys went to sleep, but later took turns awaiting the strange intruder. Throughout the night no one came near the spot.

"The thief probably won't return so long as we're here," suggested Chet. "I'm tired of this business anyway. Tonight I'm going to get a good rest in a bed."

"And leave us alone to catch the thief?" Joe winked at Frank.

After their chum had been properly apologetic, Joe explained that he and his brother had to stay at home and watch "Mr Spanish".

"Then I'll get Tony Prito here," said Chet. "I won't quit. I promise."

"That's the spirit," laughed Joe. "And let us know if anything happens."

The brothers went home. Their father had returned from New York, so after lunch the three set out for the hospital to call on "Mr Spanish".

The patient was politely grateful when Mr Hardy explained the object of their visit.

"It is most good of you," he said earnestly. "I have been wondering what I should do. It is a most awkward situation. But how can I repay you? After all, I am a stranger to you. I have no money——"

"We'll forget about that," smiled Fenton Hardy. "The main thing is for you to get well and have your memory restored. You're welcome to come and stay with us as long as you wish."

"But my clothes. When I was found lying in the street, they were muddy and torn. They have not been cleaned."

"I thought of that, and brought a suit of mine. You're just about the size to wear it. In the meantime, the boys will take yours to the tailor and have it repaired and cleaned."

It was decided that "Mr Spanish" and Fenton Hardy

would go directly home, while Frank and Joe would take the amnesia victim's suit downtown to be fixed.

"Hmm! This sure needs attention," commented the tailor a short time later, holding up the jacket. "It will take a couple of days."

He deftly turned the pockets inside out to make sure nothing of value was in them. Chief Collig already told the boys that "Mr Spanish's" clothes had been thoroughly searched for clues to his identity, and that none had been found. Frank and Joe were surprised, therefore, when the tailor pulled out something.

"Ha! What's this?"

He had turned an inner coat pocket inside out. There, in a second one sewn within the first, he had felt a hard object. The man fumbled a moment, then extracted it.

The object he held up was a coin. A gold coin.

"Better take care of that," said the tailor, handing it over to Frank. "Looks like a gold piece."

The Hardy boys were careful to show no surprise, though they were amazed at the find.

"Thanks a lot," Frank said, taking the money. "The owner will be glad to get this back. He probably forgot all about it."

The boys left the place and waited until they were round the corner before they spoke. Then they halted and excitedly examined the gold piece.

"It isn't United States money," declared Joe. "Look! What do you suppose it is?"

The coin was old. On one side was a date—1725. On the other was the likeness of a woman's face with a Spanish head-dress. The only wording on the piece, a religious motto, was in Spanish.

"It's very strange," said Joe.

"The woman's head!" exclaimed Frank. "It's the same as the one tattooed on the hold-up man's chest!"

"Are you sure?"

"Positive."

The brothers looked at each other in astonishment. They realised that this coin, so well hidden in "Mr Spanish's" secret pocket, might prove to be a valuable clue to their mysterious guest's identity. But also, it might prove the man to be someone undesirable. Was there a connection between him and the fellow with the curious tatooed design on his chest?

"Let's take this coin over to Wu Sing," Frank suggested. "Perhaps he can identify it."

The Chinaman's store was only a few streets away. The elderly man greeted the boys courteously.

"You have brought more coins perhaps?" he smiled. "I shall be glad to help my friends."

"Just one more, Wu Sing," replied Joe. "We've never seen anything like this piece. Show it to him, Frank."

The boy handed the coin to him. Wu Sing took it over to the window and examined it carefully. Looking puzzled, he opened a drawer and removed a well-thumbed book. He turned page after page, comparing pictures of coins with the unusual gold piece.

"This is most strange," he mused. "Most strange. I have no record of such a coin as this."

He held it deftly between his thumb and first finger. Then he dropped it on the counter and listened to its ring.

"It is genuine gold. My book gives no record of any 1725 Spanish coin of this kind. Mr Carter perhaps can help you."

"We'll ask him," said Frank.

The boys thanked Wu Sing for his trouble and hurried out. But instead of going to visit Mr Carter, they headed for home.

"Perhaps we're just wasting time," Joe suggested. "The thing for us to do is to show this to 'Mr Spanish'. He may be able to tell us all about it."

However, when their visitor saw the gold coin, he gazed at it in complete bewilderment.

"You say you found this in a pocket of my coat?" he asked, his accent more pronounced than usual.

"A secret inside pocket. The men who robbed you must have overlooked it."

"A strange coin," mused "Mr Spanish", examining the money. "Very strange. Very old. But no—it means nothing to me."

"Perhaps you collected coins?" suggested Frank. "This isn't the sort of gold piece the average man would carry around with him."

"Mr Spanish" sighed. "Perhaps I have been a coin collector. Who knows? But I cannot remember." He passed a hand wearily across his eyes. "This gold piece means nothing to me at all."

"I'm sorry," said Frank kindly.

The boys learned that Mr Hardy expected to be home for a few hours. Since they were not needed to watch their guest, they set out to call on Mr Carter. The numismatist was deeply interested in the coin, but he also could not identify the strange piece. Disappointed, Frank and Joe went on to see Doctor Wakefield. The elderly professor became excited when he saw the coin, but could shed no light on the mystery.

"If that coin is a genuine issue," he declared, "it must be very rare. I have no record of anything like it. As you know, the value of a coin increases with its rarity. This piece is probably worth thousands of dollars."

The boys did not tell him they were not particularly concerned about the value of the coin as a collector's item. What interested them most was the connection the coin might have with the strange case of "Mr Spanish". Frank was particularly intrigued by the curious similarity between the woman's head stamped on the coin and the woman's head tattooed on the hold-up man's chest.

"Do you think it might be a symbol of some kind?" suggested Joe, as he and his brother walked towards home. "Maybe it isn't a real coin at all—just a sort of token. Perhaps an identification disc for members of a society."

Frank thought Joe might have stumbled on a brilliant idea.

"It could be that," he agreed. "That would explain why the coin collectors haven't any record of the piece."

"In that case," continued Joe, "it could mean that 'Mr Spanish' and the tattooed man——"

"Are members of the same outfit?"

Joe nodded. Both boys were troubled. They knew there was a good chance that Joe's guess might be correct. But they did not want to think so.

"I *can't* believe it!" Frank said. " 'Mr Spanish' is a gentleman. Surely he couldn't be mixed up with anyone like that hold-up guy!"

"After all we don't know anything about our visitor. We like him, and he seems to be a fine fellow, but we could be wrong. Remember, he has lost his memory. When he is in his right mind he may be a dangerous crook."

"That's true."

The boys were passing Wu Sing's store at that particular moment. They heard an urgent tap on the window. When the Hardys looked up, they saw the elderly merchant beckoning to them from beyond the glass.

"Did you find out something about the coin, Wu Sing?" asked Frank eagerly when they went inside.

The old Chinese seemed disturbed. "No, it is not about that coin," he said. "It is something else. Please to come into the back room."

When they entered the little office, Wu Sing carefully closed the door. Then he unlocked a desk drawer.

"After you left this afternoon," he said, "I received a letter—a threatening letter. I think you should see it."

He handed the boys a sheet of paper. They read in astonishment:

Wu Sing: It will be a lot healthier for you if you keep your mouth shut about coins from now on. After this when the Hardys come round asking for information tell them to mind their own business. If you don't pay any attention to this letter you will be looking for trouble.

· 12 ·

Blackbeard

THE threatening letter to Wu Sing was crudely scrawled in pencil on cheap paper. No name was signed. Silently the Oriental showed the envelope to the Hardys. It had no postmark.

"This letter wasn't mailed," said Frank.

"No. Some unworthy person laid it on counter while I was in office," replied the Chinese.

He had no idea who that individual might have been.

"This is not good," muttered Wu Sing. "I do not wish trouble. Maybe you should not come here again."

"Have you shown this letter to the police?" asked Frank.

Wu Sing shook his head. By bringing the police into the picture, he explained, he might be creating the very trouble he wished to avoid.

"Bad men write that letter," he declared tremulously. "Better I should do as they say."

"Well, we certainly don't want to get you into hot water," Joe told him. "We'll steer clear of your place from now on. If we really need your advice, we can always reach you by phone."

Wu Sing smiled gratefully. He shook hands warmly with the boys as they left, and it was plain that he was relieved by their willingness to spare him embarrasment.

"It proves we're bothering someone," Frank said as the boys walked home. "But whom?"

"And why?" added Joe. "We don't know whether the letter referred to the coins Chet found or to this gold one."

Late that afternoon Fenton Hardy decided to make a quick trip to Washington by plane to complete plans for his business trip. He took the Spanish coin with him.

"Perhaps one of the experts down there can identify it," he told his sons. "I'll be back tomorrow. No doubt I'll have something to tell you then."

The boys spent the rest of the day at home, for Aunt Gertrude insisted that "Mr Spanish" should not be left unwatched a minute. Their guest, polite and grateful for all the kindness the Hardys had shown him, was quite unaware of the fact that he was an object of such concern. The boys entertained him with stories of some of their detective adventures, and he listened with rapt interest.

"You must be experts in—what do you say—deduction!" cried "Mr Spanish". "If you have solved other mysteries, who knows but that you can solve this mystery of mine. Who am I? Where do I come from? Why am I here?"

"We're trying, 'Mr Spanish', " Frank assured the man. "You can depend on it, we'll do the best we can."

As soon as Mr Hardy returned from Washington the next day, he told his sons that even a government expert had been unable to give him any information about the strange gold coin.

"For the time being, I'll turn 'Mr Spanish's' case over to you," he said. "See what you can make of it. Frank, give this coin back to our guest."

As Mr Hardy planned to be at home all evening,

there was no need for the boys to remain. Immediately after an early dinner they slipped out of the house.

"I have an idea," said Frank mysteriously. "It might not lead to anything, but I think it's worth trying. Come on."

He led the way through the streets of Bayport, heading towards the docks section.

"I don't get this," said Joe. "What have you in mind?"

"Tattoo marks," declared Frank. "What type of men go in for tattooing?"

"Lumberjacks and—and sailors!"

"Right. And here we are, living in a coastal city, and didn't even think of it. Ten chances to one that hold-up man is or has been a sailor. The place for us to search is along the docks."

"For a man with a Spanish woman's head tattooed on his chest?"

"Or for someone who *knows* of a man with a Spanish woman's head tattoed on his chest."

Bayport's dock area was a picturesque but squalid part of the city. The streets were dark and crooked, crowded with second-hand stores, cheap hotels, and shabby restaurants. There was an unpleasant odour of strong food in the air. Mahogany-tanned men in sea-caps and jackets strode the streets, ambling along with the rolling gait peculiar to sailors.

"Not very pleasant here," said Frank.

In front of a shabby restaurant known as The Mariner's Coffee House a car was parked. The boys had almost passed it when Frank suddenly turned and gazed at the vehicle.

"I may be wrong," he said quietly, "but this looks mighty like the hold-up man's car!"

Joe whistled softly. "Are you sure?"

"I can't be sure. I only got a glimpse of it, but this is the same make and model, same colour—and one of the side windows had a crack in it, just like this one."

Joe looked at the Mariner's Coffee House.

"Think your hold-up man may be in there?"

"Could be. Let's go in and look around."

Joe held his brother back. "If we do that and he recognizes you, he'll just clear out. Suppose I go in alone. If the man's there, he won't recognize *me*."

"How are you going to find out if he has a tattooed chest?"

"I have an idea about that. You wait round the corner and keep an eye on this car."

Joe opened the restaurant door and stepped inside. It was a noisy, smoky place. Two or three sailors were perched on stools at a counter. Others were sitting round tables at the back of the restaurant. There was a good deal of hearty talk and argument. A mechanical piano was jangling away, adding to the cheerful racket.

Joe felt a little out of his element at first, but he had resolved on the part he was to play, so he did the best he could. He pulled his hat down over one eye, swaggered up to a table and sat down. He ordered a sandwich. While waiting to be served, he noticed an elderly sailor at the next table. The man's hands were blue with tattoo marks.

"Say, old-timer," drawled Joe, "I been thinkin' of gettin' myself tattooed. Where do I go to get a good job like that one o' yours?" he asked.

The old sailor was pleased. He rolled up his sleeves and revealed a complicated design of flags and serpents on his arms.

"Can't get a job this like done here in Bayport," he

boomed. "Ain't nobody round this town can do a good tattooin' job. New York or New Orleans or Frisco, maybe. But not here."

A dark-skinned man with shifty eyes half turned round from the counter where he was eating, and listened intently. In a few moments he left by a side door, hurrying off to the next street.

Joe paid for his sandwich and carried it over to the old sailor's table. "Mind if I sit down?"

"Make yourself at home, sonny." He called over to a companion nearby, a youngish, sallow-faced man. "Steve, here's a kid says he wants a tattooin' job. I'm tellin' him to lay off these local experts. That right?"

"Sure, you're right." The sallow man lounged over and pulled open the front of his shirt. Across his chest was tattooed a partiotic design of the Statue of Liberty, completely surrounded by stars. "Now that was done in Rio. Took hours. And did it hurt! But it was worth it," he added proudly.

Most of the men in the restaurant knew one another. Everyone suddenly became personally interested in Joe's tattooing problem. They gathered round. Some advised him against being tattooed at all at his age. They said he might regret it later.

Two men gave him the addresses of tattooing experts in other coastal cities. Several revealed strange marks on their arms and chests, and launched into long stories telling how the operations had been performed.

Joe saw nothing of a tattoo design of a woman's face with a Spanish head-dress. He brought up the subject casually.

"Design I had in mind, if I ever do get tattooed, is a woman's head. Do you think a good tattoo man could put one on my chest? Something Spanish?"

"Sure—a real tattoo artist could make any design you like. Can't say I've ever seen one like the kind you mention, though," declared the old sailor.

Apparently none of the others had either. So after a while Joe said goodbye and swaggered out of the place. Round the corner he found Frank.

"Any luck?" he asked his brother eagerly.

Joe shook his head. "I learned plenty about tattooing, and saw practically every design in the place. But no Spanish woman's head."

"I wonder how that car comes to be parked here? Let's hang around for a while. If it belongs to the hold-up man, he may not have gone into the restaurant at all. He may be in some other joint nearby."

The boys sauntered along the street. At the end of it they turned and strolled back again, keeping the parked car under observation. They were nearing The Mariner's Coffee House again when a raggedly dressed boy emerged from an alley across the street and whistled to them shrilly.

"Hey—you in the blue jacket!" called out the lad to Joe. "You're wanted."

"Who wants me?"

"A man over in the next street gave me money to tell you he wants to talk to you. He says it's important. Come on—I'll show you the place."

The Hardy boys were suspicious.

"What's his name?" asked Joe.

"I dunno his name. He's a tattoo man. Hurry if you're coming."

"You'd better be careful," said Frank quietly to his brother. "It may be a trap. But I'd like to know what he wants."

They crossed the street. The lad turned swiftly and

led them down a dark alley into the next street, then into another alley. There he halted in front of a shabby little building, and beckoned to the boys.

"Come on," he called shrilly. "This is it. The man's waitin'."

"I don't like the looks of this place," muttered Joe, "but I'll go in. You'd better stay outside and watch, Frank," he whispered.

"Don't you think we'd better stick together?"

"If I'm not out in ten minutes, you'll know something is wrong, and can get help."

"Right." Frank turned and walked slowly down the alley.

"What's the matter with him? Ain't he coming?" demanded the lad, who was waiting at the top of the steps.

"No. Where is this tattoo man who wants to see me?"

The boy opened the door and went inside. Joe followed him into a squalid, foul-smelling place. The windows were dirty. The walls were stained and grimy. In a cluttered front room a faded, hand-lettered sign on the wall proclaimed:

"Expert Tattooing Done Here. Rates Cheap."

Near the door stood a half-naked, dark-skinned man. After telling the lad to wait outside, this strange person turned to Joe and said:

"My master is ready."

He opened a door to an inner room. Joe gasped in astonishment. At a table sat an immense, coarse-featured man, with a long, bushy black beard. He was dressed in pirate's clothes, and in his belt were stuck a long knife and cutlass.

The fellow's shirt sleeves were rolled up to the elbows, exposing muscular arms traced with a multitude of blue tattoo marks.

"See them!" boomed the swarthy man, holding out his arm. "You ever see a tattooing job like that? Well, don't let anybody tell you a good job can't be done right here in Bayport. I'm as good as any artist in the business, see, and don't let anyone tell you different."

Joe realized that somehow or other word had come to this queer individual from the Mariner's Coffee House that the boy wanted to be tattooed.

"And why shouldn't I be an artist at putting pictures on the human body that will stay on forever? I'm a descendant of Blackbeard. You've heard of Blackbeard, ain't you?"

"Blackbeard the pirate?"

"The same. Bravest pirate that ever sailed the seven seas. My ancestor, him."

Joe gulped. He recalled that Blackbeard was known to have been the cruellest and most ferocious of all the pirates who plundered and tortured in the waters of the Caribbean. If this person before Joe truly were a descendant of this monster, anything might happen!

"I'll try to get a look at his chest and see if that tattoo mark with the Spanish woman's head is on there," thought Joe. "Then I'll get out of here as fast as I can."

"Yes, I'm Blackbeard the pirate too," gloated the man at the table. "And they say I look like my ancestor."

"Are your tattoo marks the same as his?" asked Joe.

"Dunno," said Blackbeard. "But I got some fine ones. Especially the picture on my chest."

The boy's heart thumped as the man tore open his shirt front. His chest was a weird conglomeration of writhing blue snakes entwined about a ship under full sail.

"Ain't that wonderful?" cried Blackbeard.

Joe admired the work, then started for the door. This was not the man who held up Frank.

"Now look, sonny—you want to be tattooed," Blackbeard reminded him. "Well, I'm your man. And it won't cost you much either. Twenty-five dollars, and if you know anything about tattooing, you got to admit that's dirt cheap. In the big cities it would cost you twice as much."

Joe was evasive. "I'm not sure I want the job done right away. I'll let you know."

"I'll make it ten dollars."

"Well, I'll think it over," said Joe, suspicious now, and becoming anxious that he might not get away unmarked.

But Blackbeard was not to be put off so easily. He suddenly leaped up and lunged round the table. He seized Joe by the collar.

"Not so fast," he growled menacingly. "You said you wanted to be tattooed, and you're going to be tattooed!"

13

The Police Hunt

JOE began to struggle. But Blackbeard was strong and powerful.

"I'll tattoo you if it's the last thing I do! I'll do it for nothing!" He raised his voice, shouting, "Lopez! Come here!"

A door opened. The servant rushed in and flung himself at Joe. Against the two men the boy was helpless.

"Quick!" panted Blackbeard.

Joe tried to shout, but the pirate's heavy hand was across his mouth, stifling any outcry. He fought with all his strength, but Lopez produced a length of rope and whipped it round the boys ankles. In a few minutes he was bound, gagged, and thrust on to a table.

"Get the needle, Lopez!" ordered Blackbeard.

The servant scuttled into another room. The pirate, his heavy arms folded, looked at Joe with a satisfied air. Then he reached down and ripped open the boy's shirt.

Joe was utterly helpless, yet he struggled grimly against the ropes that bound him. Lopez returned and handed Blackbeard a long, sharp needle in a holder. Joe felt a stab of pain as the tattoo artist crouched over him and the needle pricked the skin on his chest.

"You'll get a design you maybe never heard of before," grunted Blackbeard. "First, I prick the design. Then comes the dye."

The sharp needle stabbed Joe's skin again.

"*I'll put the Curse of the Caribbees on you!*" muttered Blackbeard.

The Hardy boy wondered if he had heard right. The very expression "Mr Spanish" had uttered! Was the man at their house mixed up with this horrible-looking creature?

"The mark will stay with you for life," cried the pirate. "And my days of bad luck will be gone for ever! Lopez, send for the other boy!"

In the meantime, Frank had been on watch in the street at the end of the alley. Although after ten minutes he was worried because his brother had not appeared, he decided to wait a few moments longer. During this time, the car he suspected of belonging to the hold-up man, passed him. A girl was driving, and there were no other passengers.

"Well, that's that," thought Frank.

When fifteen minutes had gone by, and there was still no sign of Joe, he determined to go for help, when suddenly out of the alley came the same lad who had guided the Hardys over from the other street.

"Look here," Frank demanded. What's happened to my brother?"

"Keep your shirt on," retorted the boy impudently. "I just came out to look for you. Your brother said you were to meet him at the other end of the alley."

Frank felt relieved. Unsuspecting, he followed the lad. He had gone not more than twenty feet when a door opened. A shadowy figure sprang into the alley and pounced on him.

Frank's cry of alarm was muffled by a heavy hand being clapped over his mouth. There was a brief, unequal struggle. The boy fled into the shadows, his treacherous work done. Frank was dragged inside the building and the door slammed shut. The alley was deserted.

Back on the street, across from the Mariner's Coffee Shop, another man had been watching the Hardy boys during their visit to the dock area. He was an old Chinese laundryman with twinkling, friendly eyes.

While ironing shirts at the window of his tiny place of business, he had seen and recognized the brothers. The fact that they were friends of Wu Sing, who was a respected and powerful figure in the life of Bayport's Chinese community, aroused his interest.

When the old laundryman saw the boys follow the raggedly dressed lad, who was known in the harbour area as a tout for gambling dens where sailors were sometimes beaten and robbed, he left his ironing board and stole out to investigate.

After looking up and down various streets, and seeing no sign of Frank and Joe, he telephoned Wu Sing. After this call, Wu Sing rang the Bayport Police Department.

"I am afraid the Hardy boys may be in trouble in the dock area," he said. "I think perhaps you should go there quickly and find out."

When the message was relayed to Chief Collig, he wasted no time. He immediately ordered a car, and three policemen began a systematic search of the area pointed out by the laundryman. But there was no sign of the Hardys.

"The boy you saw take them away. Who was he?" the Chief asked the laundryman.

"His name Sammy. Bad boy."

"I know him," said the chief, "and the sooner we

get a hold of him the better. We'll concentrate on trying to find the lad."

Immediately he detailed two of his men to search the alley for Sammy, and before the lad could escape from either end, the two policemen were running towards him, one from each direction. Sammy dodged into a yard, but his freedom was short-lived. He was caught hiding behind a barrel.

"Where are those boys you brought here?" demanded one of the officers.

"Dunno."

"Oh, yes you do. Now look here, Sammy, tell me where the boys are."

Sammy would say nothing, but he rolled his eyes towards a house across the alley.

"In there?" whispered his captor.

Chief Collig and the fourth policeman had arrived. Sammy knew the game was up.

"Yes," he gulped. "They're in the house of the guy with the black beard."

While a policeman held the lad tightly, the others strode to the door of the shabby house. Chief Collig ordered one of the men round to the rear of the building, while he knocked loudly on the front entrance. No one answered. He tried to open the door. It was locked.

"Break it in!" snapped the chief.

His men threw their shoulders against the flimsy structure. Hinges creaked and snapped at the first impact. At the second onslaught the wood splintered and caved in with a resounding crash. The police stormed inside.

A brief glance told them the front room was empty. They surged quickly into the tiny one at the back.

14

A Valuable Letter

FRANK HARDY lay on a couch, bound and gagged. Joe had been left lying across the table. Blackbeard and his sinister servant Lopez had vanished.

The Hardys were released quickly. They had suffered no real injuries. Fortunately for Joe, the pirate had not had time to go very far with the tattooing, and there were just pinpricks on the boy's chest.

"After this," growled Chief Collig, "when you two boys decide on doing a little detective work down in this part of town, let us know in advance. If Wu Sing hadn't tipped us off, you might have been in a bad fix."

"Wu Sing!" exclaimed Frank in astonishment. "How did he know where we were?"

"From my very good friend," said a voice in the doorway.

The group turned to see Wu Sing and the laundryman standing there. Both were relieved to find the boys unharmed. Before anyone could thank them, however, the men bowed and vanished.

"Just like them," smiled Frank.

Collig ordered one of the policemen to take Sammy to headquarters. Then he turned to the Hardys, telling them he would drive them home.

"How did you get into this mess?" he asked the boys as they drove along. "Better own up. We don't want any more trouble."

The brothers explained how they had thought that

the man who had held up Frank might be a sailor because of the picture on his chest, and of how they had been lured into Blackbeard's house trying to find him.

"Blackbeard, huh?" said Collig. "We'll try to pick him up. Never heard of him, or of Lopez, either."

"They'll probably sneak on board a ship and we'll never see them again," grunted one of the policemen.

Joe had not revealed that the man who called himself a descendant of a famous pirate had said he was going to transfer *The Curse of the Caribbees* to him. He did tell his brother and his father, however, as soon as they reached home.

In the privacy of his study Mr Hardy listened intently to the whole story of his sons' adventure.

"Well, you both have been very lucky, that's all I can say," he observed, when they had finished. "You might have run into very serious trouble. I think I'll call up Wu Sing and thank him."

Mr Hardy expressed his appreciation to the Chinese merchant, and asked that the laundryman also be thanked.

When the detective replaced the telephone receiver, he turned to his sons. "From what you tell me, I'm inclined to believe Blackbeard is insane."

"He certainly didn't act like a normal person," agreed Joe.

"Maybe he is mixed up with some gang," offered Frank, "and isn't crazy at all."

"True. While he is at large, I think you two boys had better take extra precautions," said his father.

"We might go out to Chet Morton's place for a few days," said Joe, wondering what his friend might have unearthed since he and his brother had left the farm.

"What about 'Mr Spanish'? " asked Frank. "Who would watch him?"

"I can get a plain-clothes man here any time I go away," his father replied. "Go ahead to Chet's. It's a good idea. And now I believe we should talk to 'Mr Spanish'. That remark of Blackbeard's about the *Curse of the Caribbees* may have some significance for him."

The strange guest was called into the conference. He listened with grave interest while the boys told him about their evening's adventure.

"Blackbeard? Lopez?" the man said finally.

He closed his eyes, vainly trying to remember. Then he regarded his friends helplessly.

"It is stupid of me. I am sorry, but I can remember nothing. About the coin found in my pocket, I remember nothing. About the *Curse of the Caribbees*—if I said something regarding it when I was in hospital, I do not remember. It means nothing to me. No—none of this brings anything to my mind."

"Well, don't worry about it," advised Fenton Hardy kindly. "Everything will probably come back to you before long. You may wake up some morning and remember your whole past life, as clear as daylight."

"I hope so," said "Mr Spanish" sadly. "It is a terrible thing to lose one's past."

The next morning, the boys set out to stay at the Morton farmhouse. They arrived at the front gate just in time to overhear Chet's father delivering a strong lecture to the crestfallen boy.

"Never in all my life have I seen anything like it!" declared Mr Morton wrathfully. "I thought there was something suspicious. I never knew you to work like that before. But why in the world, when I give you a simple little task to do, you can't just go and do it without making such an infernal mess, is more than I can understand."

"Well, I kind of got working on something else," murmured Chet apologetically.

"I should say you did. What were you trying to do—dig a canal?"

Mr Morton looked up at that moment and saw the Hardys grinning gleefully at their chum's discomfiture.

"Come on in, boys," he said cheerfully. Then he appealed to them. "Did you see what this son of mine has done to that field? I ask him to dig a ditch. Just an ordinary, simple little ditch that shouldn't have taken more than two or three hours.

"And what happens while I'm away? He works morning and night. He even camps down there. He sleeps and eats there. I came home last night and this morning I went down to see what he had done. And what do I find?" Mr Morton's voice rose plaintively. "I discover that he's gone and dug up half my field. It's a mess."

"I guess maybe we were partly to blame," said Frank.

Mr Morton was not inclined to believe this. "Don't try to share the blame. You boys have good sense. You wouldn't go digging holes all over the place if you were asked merely to dig a ditch. But this son of mine—he makes an excavation job out of it." He turned to Chet again. "What *were* you up to, anyway?"

Chet gulped miserably.

"Better tell your father about it, Chet," suggested Frank.

"Do you mean to say there *is* an explanation? That it wasn't just plain nonsense?" demanded Mr Morton.

Chet gulped again.

"I—I was digging for buried treasure," he faltered.

"Buried treasure!" cried Mr Morton. "Now I've

heard everything. What on earth possessed you to dig for buried treasure down there?"

"Because I found some," muttered Chet.

He fished out the old coins from his pocket and handed them to his father.

"That's true, Mr Morton," spoke up Joe. "We've been helping Chet. We were keeping the hunt a secret."

Mr Morton examined the coins. His manner suddenly changed.

"This is odd," he said quietly. "Very odd. Buried treasure, eh? Do you mean to tell me you found these when you were digging the ditch?"

"Both of them," said Chet.

The fat boy's father looked up. "Well," he said, "that's different. Why didn't you tell me about this before? Because now I can tell *you* a secret. I've done a little treasure-hunting on this property myself, but I kept quiet about it because I thought the whole thing probably was a hoax."

Chet's eyes bulged.

"Dad, do you mean to say you *know* there's treasure buried somewhere round here?"

"I can't say I know for sure. But since you've actually found these old coins, maybe there's something to it after all."

Mr Morton went on to say that shortly after he had bought the farm, he did some repair work on the house. While tearing down a wall that was in bad condition he had discovered among the debris a small tin box which evidently had been hidden in the wall.

"The box contained an old letter," continued Mr Morton. "A letter which told about a certain treasure that was to be buried somewhere on the property.

Frank and Joe looked at each other. Mr Morton's

story had put a totally new light on things; not only on the idea of a treasure buried long ago, but also on the Hardys' assumption that a thief had buried loot there recently. Now it looked as if the intruder had been digging for the treasure. Since he had not returned, there came again the harrowing thought: had he found it?

"Did the letter say the treasure was in the field by the brook?" asked Chet hopefully.

"It merely said the treasure was in a field, but didn't say which field. I can remember plainly the directions it gave. Ten paces west of the oak tree, four paces south to the white boulder, then seven paces east on a line with the brook.

"I did my digging in the field at the north boundary of the property, up by the head of the brook. There were a lot of white boulders there at the time, and I thought one of them might be the marker."

Chet was greatly excited. Gone were his doubts about the existence of the treasure.

"Come on!" he yelled to Frank and Joe. "We're on the right trail now. Let's get back to digging again!"

"I'll get the letter," declared Mr Morton enthusiastically, starting for the house. "You boys go on down to the field."

On the way Frank asked Chet if Tony had come out to help him.

"No, he's working for his father. But I kept an eye on things!" he added proudly.

When Mr Morton and the boys gathered by the brook about fifteen minutes later, the three chums gazed at the ancient letter in awe. The sheet was about ready to fall apart at the places where it had been creased. The nk had faded so much that the words were barely discernible.

"It must be very old," remarked Frank. "A hundred years or more."

"Yes," agreed Mr Morton, "but how valuable? That's the important thing."

"If the coins we found are part of the treasure, maybe the letter is much older," said Chet.

"That's not likely," guessed Joe, "because your house isn't more than a hundred years old, is it, Mr Morton?"

"The letter could have been taken there from an older house on the place," Chet insisted.

"Well, let's get started. We begin at an oak tree," said his father.

The boys went immediately to the only oak tree that grew near the brook.

"Now 'ten paces west', " read Mr Morton.

His son measured the distance.

" 'Four paces south to the white boulder'. "

This was not so easy, for the only large stone in sight was a little farther away than the directions stated.

"It probably moved," declared Chet, undaunted by this delay.

"And now 'seven paces east on a line with the brook';" said Mr Morton.

His son paced off the seven steps, came to a halt, and looked at his father.

"If we dig round here," the man said, "I believe we should be reasonably near the spot."

Spades were produced. Chet's father, who had been scolding his boy not half an hour before for the amount of excavation work that had been done on the meadow, was soon digging with as much enthusiasm as the others. Earth flew in all directions for several minutes. Then Chet cried out suddenly:

"Stop! Wait a minute!"

· 15 ·

The Hidden Pit

"I've FOUND something," puffed Chet, reaching into the hole he had dug.

Red in the face and with teeth clenched, the youth at last succeeded in unearthing what looked like a box but it proved to be only a stone, rust in colour and nearly square in shape.

"Aw gee, I thought I had the treasure," groaned Chet, wiping perspiration from his forehead. "I guess we aren't digging in the right place."

"You mustn't get discouraged so easily," advised his father.

But after an hour of hard work under the hot sun, even Mr Morton began to reconcile himself to disappointment and defeat. They had discovered nothing.

"Maybe we're in the wrong field," suggested Frank hopefully. "Perhaps the boulder mentioned in the letter is in another place."

"The course of the brook may have changed since the directions were written," added Joe.

Mr Morton rested wearily on the handle of his spade and looked round.

"Maybe I was right the first time in thinking that the letter is a hoax," he said.

Chet held to the opinion that the letter was genuine, and that they were looking in the wrong spot.

"You boys will have to carry on alone," said Mr

"I've found it!" cried Chet

Morton. "Treasure or no treasure, I have to get back to my work."

He took the two old coins from his pocket and handed them to Frank.

"Suppose you show these to your father," he said. Then he wagged a finger at Chet. "No more secrets from me, young man. If you find anything that looks like a clue to buried money, I want to know about it."

Chet promised faithfully to keep his father informed of everything that happened in the treasure hunt from then on. After the man had gone up to the farmhouse the boys began to search the other fields, but found neither oak trees nor white boulders.

"We don't even know if that letter refers to this farm," said Joe. "It might have been brought here from some distant place."

"But how about that guy who was digging here one night?" asked Chet. "He must have known about it. Otherwise why would he have knocked me out? He probably was afraid that I would find the treasure."

"I still think," maintained Frank, "that the fellow who attacked you wasn't concerned with treasure. He was trying to find some loot he had buried round here."

"You mean lately?"

"Yes. Something he probably stole in Bayport quite recently."

The Hardy boy had reached into his pocket, and drew out a map of the Bayport area.

"What are you looking for?" asked Joe.

"I have an idea," said Frank. "Suppose that fellow who slugged Chet was the one who attacked 'Mr Spanish', and took cash, paper money, even jewellery from him."

"Yes. What of it?" asked Joe.

"Where does a thief usually hide after a robbery?" asked Frank.

"The place where he lives," replied Chet. "Or where his pals hang out."

"Precisely."

Frank took a pencil from his pocket and drew a straight line from the exact spot where "Mr Spanish" had been waylaid, through the Morton farm, and on into the country. It came to a place called Hixon.

"You think the thief lives in Hixon?" Joe asked.

"That's my guess," said Frank. "But I also think he buried the loot somewhere along the route on his way home. What say we follow the trail indicated by this pencil line? If the thief hasn't already found what he was digging for, maybe we shall!"

"I believe you've got something there," cried Joe. "If we don't find the loot, at least we may find the thief." Then another thought struck him. "But how would you recognize him if you did meet him?"

"I don't know," confessed Frank, "but it may be that it's the same fellow who held me up."

"Let's go!" cried Joe, eager for action. "You lead the way."

The three boys started off in a westerly direction. They reached the far fence that bordered the Morton farm without finding any spot that might suggest a hiding place for loot. After climbing the fence, they set off in the direction of Hixon.

"That map idea of yours is all right, providing the thief walked in a straight line," objected Chet wearily. "But what if he didn't?"

"We'll have to take our chances on that," replied Frank. "If he was in a hurry to hide his loot, he wouldn't wander all over the countryside."

They had gone about a hundred yards farther when Chet spied a large, greyish rock in the grass some distance ahead.

"Say, that might be the white boulder mentioned in the old letter," he cried excitedly. "Your idea is all right, Frank, but after all a buried treasure is more interesting."

"The boulder isn't very white," Joe remarked.

"It could have been a few years ago."

"It's too small for a boulder. And there's no oak tree near it."

But Chet was not to be discouraged so easily. He raced ahead to investigate the rock. Suddenly he skidded to a stop.

"Hey! Come quick!" he shouted back. "This looks like something."

The Hardys sped to join him. What Chet had come upon was a shallow depression in the ground.

"I'll bet the treasure is here!" he cried, and hurried back across the fence to get a shovel.

When the Hardys examined the spot carefully, they saw that some of the grass was dry and dead.

"Almost looks as if the turf had been dug up lately and then put back," remarked Joe to his brother.

"Earth does sink like this when a hole is dug and then filled in again."

"I'm sure the treasure isn't here, but maybe the loot is!" said Frank excitedly. "The place is worth investigating."

In a few minutes Chet returned with a shovel and started to attack the depression in the earth.

"Yes, sir, I'll bet this is it. I wonder how much the treasure is worth. Thousands of dollars, likely. Oh, boy, just wait till I go up to the house and tell Dad I found the buried treasure!"

"You haven't found it yet," Joe reminded his chum.

"I will!" declared Chet confidently. He stepped back, put down his spade, and rubbed his hands together gleefully. "Yep!" the stout boy declared blithely, "I think I've fallen right into it this time——"

Suddenly Chet seemed to lose his balance. He did a wild war dance trying to steady himself. Then the ground dropped from beneath his feet. There was a splintering crash, and he disappeared from view.

The brothers rushed to the brink of the hole.

"Chet!" yelled Joe. "Are you all right?"

From below came a wheezy gasp, followed by a splutter and a cough.

"G-get me out of here!"

The pit was about three feet across. The Hardys suddenly realized the sides might cave in and engulf their chum, but on investigation they found that the earth round the hole was solid. The walls were lined with stones. The boys peered down, but could not see their friend because splintered boards were sticking out from the sides of the pit.

"I think I've broken my neck!" groaned Chet. "Lower a rope, somebody, and pull me out of here quick!"

In a moment he struggled to his feet, and reported, to the others' relief, that he was unharmed. He was only about ten feet below the surface, but when Frank and Joe tried to reach him, they found it impossible.

Joe sped back to the tent for a length of rope. Frank stretched out on the grass at the top of the pit, and kept up Chet's courage by assuring him that rescue would be only a matter of minutes.

"What in the world do you suppose this hole is anyhow?" asked the fat boy. "It looks like a well, but it isn't deep enough, and there's no water."

"Those are broken boards above you, aren't they?" asked Frank.

"I must have crashed through a platform. There probably was loose dirt and turf on top of it, so I couldn't see the boards. My weight was too much for them."

"Good reason for reducing," grinned Frank. "Any treasure down there?"

"I don't feel anything," Chet called back after groping around. "It's too dark to see, though. But when I fell in, I was sure I heard something hard land ahead of me."

Frank was thinking fast. A stone-lined hole, a platform—he remembered a story he had once read about some pirates who had buried their loot at various levels of a pit by building a series of wooden platforms at different heights. On each of these they had laid a part of their treasure and piled dirt over it all.

Anyone finding the topmost hiding-place, which always held the least in value, would conclude that he had found all the treasure. Frank wondered if this pit might be an ingenious hiding-place of this kind. He also immediately thought of the pirate Blackbeard and his tattooing descendant.

Joe came scurrying back with the rope, and the Hardys lowered it to Chet. After much puffing and pulling, their chum was hauled to the surface, where he lay gasping on the grass.

"Gosh, that was a narrow squeak! Lucky I wasn't buried alive!" he grunted. "No more pits for me!"

"What do you mean? Aren't you going down there again to look for the treasure?" Joe gibed him.

"Not me," puffed the rescued boy, but in a moment he changed his mind.

Frank outlined his theory of the platforms and the

pit levels. Joe was impressed, and Chet's eyes bulged.

"You mean maybe some pirates built this thing?" he gasped.

Frank shrugged, and began looping the rope underneath his arms. "I'm going down to find out if anything has been hidden there, either long ago or recently."

"It's too dark to see anything," Chet warned him.

"I happen to have a torch," grinned Frank. "Come on, boys. Grab hold of this rope and lower away."

He advanced to the edge of the pit and let himself over the side. While the others paid out the rope, Frank descended past the broken platform. Down at the bottom at last he turned on the torch, and began his investigation.

The walls were of solid stone, well built. It was possible the place had originally been a well which had dried up. Perhaps the platform had been added recently by someone who knew the story of this method of hiding loot.

"Find anything?" shouted Joe.

"Not yet." Frank's voice was muffled. "But it sure looks as if this pit was made for some good reason."

He now tackled the debris of loose dirt and shattered boards which lay on the floor of the pit, but his search revealed nothing. Above, Chet was growing nervous, fearing for his chum's safety.

"For all you know, you may be standing on *another* platform right now," he shouted down. "If the floor should cave in, we might never get you out. Better give up and come back. Your father and mother wouldn't—"

Suddenly Frank called out. There was a note of excitement in his voice.

"I think I've—yes!" he cried. "Haul away, fellows! *I've found something!*"

· 16 ·

The Leather Pouch

CHET and Joe hauled wildly at the rope to pull Frank from the pit. He was soon at the top. In his arms he held a leather pouch.

"Treasure!" whooped Chet, almost letting go the rope in h s excitement.

The pouch, large and heavy, was tied with a leather thong. Joe opened it and peered inside.

"What is it? What is it?" babbled Chet.

Joe dug his hand in and produced a palm full of coins. Chet gave a loud cheer. Frank grabbed the pouch and turned it upside down, dumping its contents on the ground. In awe the boys gazed upon several hundred coins; some gold, some silver.

"We've ound the long-buried treasure!" shouted Chet. "Hey, what's the matter with you, Joe?"

The other was examining the money in his hand. Then he looked at the pile on the ground.

"That's funny," he said. "There's nothing on these coins. I can't tell what kind of coins they are. The impressions have been melted off them."

This was true. Each piece in the heap was merely a disc of metal, dateless and faceless, with every clue to its identification erased. The boys sorted them out. Not a coin had been overlooked in the melting process.

"Why would anybody do that?" asked Chet, bewildered by the discovery.

"So the coins couldn't be traced if they had been stolen," Joe answered.

"But they're no good this way," objected his fat chum.

"No, but they could be melted into a big lump of gold or silver and sold."

"Or restamped by a counterfeiter," added Frank.

"You mean to say some thief planned to do such a thing a couple of hundred years ago?" Chet asked.

"No," said Frank. "The fellow who had these coins put them here recently. This leather pouch is new."

In dismay Chet looked at the bag and had to agree.

"Here I thought the buried treasure was mine, and now—Say," he said, "how do you explain this pit? Don't tell me your thief dug such a big hole for just one little bag of coins!"

"The pit must have been constructed a long time ago," said Frank slowly. "Maybe your treasure was buried there and someone dug it up recently. The thief may even have melted off the markings on the coins he found and then put them back here in a new bag."

"I'll bet there's a lot more money down in this hole," said Chet, cheerful again. "How about that idea of the platforms?" he asked. "Perhaps the one I fell through *is* just the first of several. Even if these coins aren't part of the treasure, the stuff mentioned in the letter may be hidden down there."

The boys talked things over. It was decided that since Joe had not been down at all, he should be the one to go. He picked up the rope and a shovel. The other two lowered him carefully into the pit.

On the floor Joe rummaged through the debris, then began digging for another platform. After a while he gave the order to haul up. When he scrambled back to the surface, he shook his head.

"Solid bottom," he reported. "Just earth and rocks. There was only one platform and only one pouch. We've found all there was to find."

"Now I don't know whether these coins are the treasure we're looking for or not," sighed Chet. "Let's take them up to the house and show them to Dad."

"All right, but first I'd like to investigate something else. Suppose you go on up to the house, Chet. I want to follow the line on this map and see if I can get any clues to the man we want to locate."

"I'll go with you," offered Joe.

Chet trundled off to see his father, while the Hardys searched the ground and also several farm buildings which were on the route. They found nothing. Presently they came to the small town of Hixon.

"Let's ask a few questions round here and see what we can find out," suggested Frank. "We might get wind of someone with a Spanish woman's head tattooed on his chest."

"That's right," agreed Joe. "And there might be someone who collects coins or is interested in them in some special way."

The brothers separated and combed the town for information. An hour later they met at a restaurant. Each one reported total failure.

"I guess my idea wasn't so good," Frank conceded. "Well, let's get back to the Mortons."

"Before we do," said Joe, "I'll phone home and see if there's any news. Maybe 'Mr Spanish' has regained his memory."

Such was not the case, as the boy learned from Aunt Gertrude. She had other information, however.

"I suppose you and Frank will have to come traipsing back here," she said.

"What's happened, Aunty?" asked Joe.

"Plenty. Mr Carter's coin collection has been stolen. He wants to see you boys right away."

"We'll get there as fast as we can!"

Joe hung up, hurried to Frank, and reported what he had just heard.

"How are we going to get to Bayport?" his brother groaned. "There's no train or bus from here, and we haven't a car or a bicycle."

"If my eyes don't fail me, we'll go there by van." said Joe.

Down the street came an empty vehicle from the Prito Construction Company. On the driver's seat sat the Hardy boys' friend Tony, who worked for his father when he was not at school.

"Hey!" yelled Joe.

Tony grinned and pulled up at the kerb. "Want a ride? Free service to Bayport."

"You bet we do."

The brothers climbed aboard and soon they were home. Tony dropped them off near Mr Carter's house where they found him talking to Chief Collig.

"It was the hobby of a lifetime," the collector was saying sadly. "I spent many years collecting those coins. Now they're gone. I suppose I'll never see them again."

"Don't give up hope," said the officer. "We'll do our best to recover them."

The boys were told the story of the theft. Mr Carter had gone to bed the previous night after having spent a quiet hour rearranging his collection. The coins had been locked in a cabinet in his library.

That morning he had found the cabinet door forced open and the collection gone. The thief or thieves had gained access by forcing one of the library windows.

"All we have to work on are a few footprints," said Chief Collig to the Hardys. "But we'll solve the case."

"I'd like to see the footprints," said Frank. "Do they match any you have on record, Chief?"

Collig replied that they did not. He led the way outside and paused before the library window. A flower bed close to the side of the house revealed two marks.

"The thief had to step in soft earth," the chief pointed out. "That was a break for us. Those footprints may land him in jail."

Frank was down on his hands and knees examining the marks. Suddenly he straightened up and pulled something from his pocket.

"What's that?" asked Collig.

"Impressions of footprints I made a few days ago. Remember I brought them to headquarters?"

Collig grew red in the face. He watched in embarrassment as the boy compared the two sets of prints. They matched perfectly.

"Well, I have to give you credit," said the chief. "But I don't know what good this information is going to do us. Where'd you see these footprints the first time?"

"On Chet Morton's farm," replied Frank. "One night somebody knocked our friend out in a field. We've been trying to find the fellow ever since. This was the only clue we had. Now I'm certain he is a thief."

"I'll call up some of the police departments in neighbouring towns and tell them to be on the lookout for anybody selling old coins," said the officer.

"How about Doctor Wakefield's collection?" Joe suggested. "The professor may be next on the list if the thief is still in town."

"That's so," agreed Collig. "I'll find out if he's had any trouble."

"Perhaps it wouldn't be a bad idea to keep an eye on his house," suggested Joe. "You might catch the thief red-handed."

"Just what I had in mind," declared the chief hastily. "You took the words out of my mouth. I'll set a trap. I'll have this case cleared up in a few hours."

Frank and Joe winked at each other. After the officer had gone back to headquarters, the younger boy said:

"If there's any excitement around Doctor Wakefield's place, I'd like to be in on it. Jerry Gilroy's house is just across the street from the doctor's. Let's ask Jerry to let us watch from a front window."

Frank was enthusiastic about the idea. He thought no one would come until after dark, so the boys went home for a while, instead of to Chet's. They telephoned him, however, telling him about the matching footprints.

"Maybe the fellow who knocked you out will be caught tonight," Joe informed his chum enthusiastically.

"Gee, I sure hope so," replied Chet.

He went on to say that his father had gone out, and so he had not had the chance to show him the melted coins. Chet promised to go back to the field and stay on guard.

After darkness had fallen that night, the Hardy boys slipped from the house and hurried over to Jerry Gilroy's. Jerry readily agreed to let them use the living-room as an observation post, and offered to help. The three took up positions behind the curtains, where they could see what was going on across the street.

For a while nothing happened. Then Frank suddenly nudged his brother.

"Look who's coming!"

Down the street shuffled a bearded, bespectacled old man. He glanced neither to right nor to left.

"Looks like Ratchy!" exclaimed Joe.

They watched the old fellow's progress along the pavement. On reaching the Wakefield house, he turned in at the front and slowly climbed the porch steps. They saw him stand for a few moments at the door. Then it was opened by Doctor Wakefield and the caller went inside.

Ratchy's visit was very brief, soon the door of the house opened again. Apparently Doctor Wakefield did not show his visitor out, for the caller himself closed the door.

He crossed the veranda. Slowly he came down the steps and plodded off up the street.

"Probably called on Doctor Wakefield to have another look at his collection," said Frank.

"And nothing happened," added Jerry in disgust. "Why couldn't we have a robbery or something? This street is so peaceful, I believe a little excitement would be a good thing for it."

"Nevertheless, it's queer the way Ratchy keeps popping up whenever we're suspicious of something," Frank remarked.

The boys watched the old man as he disappeared from view into the darkness beyond the corner street light.

"Shall we go home?" Joe asked his brother. "I guess Doctor Wakefield's collection is safe enough."

"Let's wait a while longer," pleaded Frank.

Another minute passed. Then abruptly the silence of the deserted street was broken by the shrill blast of a police whistle!

· 17 ·

The Second Burglary

As soon as the whistle sounded, the Hardy boys saw a dark figure emerge from the shrubbery in the front of the Wakefield house and race down a path towards the back.

"Come on!" shouted Joe, leading the way. "This looks like action."

The three boys leaped down the steps and tore across the street. As they ran, they heard two men talking excitedly in the back garden of the Wakefield place.

"Bit me!" cried one. "Bit my hand as soon as I blew my whistle."

Frank and Joe realized that the two men were detectives from the Bayport police force, posted there by Chief Collig to guard against any attempt to steal Doctor Wakefield's coin collection.

"What happened?" shouted Frank.

"I was watching the rear of the house, when a fellow sneaked down the side path and began working at the cellar door with a skeleton key," said Detective Gibbs, nursing an injured hand. "I blew my whistle to warn Casey, who was watching the front of the place. The moment I whistled, a dog rushed out from nowhere and bit me."

"I think we'd better chase that fellow," grumbled Casey.

"I tried to catch him before he went over the fence,"

said Gibbs. "But I missed," he added ruefully. "You can chase him if you want to, but Collig said to stay here."

Frank had a sudden thought. He remembered the episode at the Hardy home, when the house was entered while everyone was distracted by the dog fight.

"While we're standing here talking," he exclaimed, "perhaps the real thief is making off with Doctor Wakefield's coin collection."

He ran up the back steps and tried the rear door. It was locked; but in a moment the professor opened it. Frank, followed closely by the other boys, hurried into the house.

"What's going on here?" demanded the old coin collector, who had on a dressing gown over his pyjamas. "A man can't get to sleep in this neighbourhood any more without being kept awake by the racket. Whistles, dogs, people shouting——"

"Your coin collection, Doctor!" said Frank. "Is it safe?"

Doctor Wakefield blinked at him in surprise.

"Why shouldn't it be safe? I locked it up just before I went to bed. It's in a cabinet in the living-room."

He turned and led the way towards the front of the house. When he entered the living-room he gasped, then cried out:

"My collection! It's gone!"

The cabinet had been forced open. The valuable coins had disappeared.

Detectives Gibbs and Casey had followed the boys into the house. Now they looked dumbfounded and crestfallen.

"But how could anyone steal the collection from under our noses?" demanded Gibbs plaintively. "I was watching the back door like a hawk, and Casey was watching the front." He glared at his colleague. "You, Casey!" he thundered. "Somebody must have got past you."

"Nobody went in the front door except an old man calling on the doctor, and he stayed only a minute."

"We saw him," said Joe.

"That was Mr Ratchy," explained Professor Wakefield. "He wanted to see the coins, but I told him I was ready for bed and he'd have to come some other time."

"Let's see if the front door is unlocked," suggested Frank. "He may have slipped the latch and sneaked in here while all of us were at the back."

The boys investigated the front door. Sure enough, the latch had been fixed!

Doctor Wakefield was greatly upset by this loss. The boys did their best to console him, telling the elderly man that at least they had a clue to the thief. They gave the two detectives a complete description of Ratchy before they left.

"We'll get him," declared Gibbs confidently. "Now that we know who he is, how can we miss?"

After the Hardys had thanked Jerry Gilroy for his help and were on their way home, Frank pointed out that various elements of the coin case were beginning to dovetail.

"I think the man who sneaked into our house and the thief who stole Doctor Wakefield's collection are either in league, or the same man working with associates. The scheme was carried out the same way both times. They staged a disturbance at the back of the house to take everyone away from the front."

"I believe you're right." Joe agreed.

It was late when the boys reached home, so they did not have a chance to show Chet's coins to their father, or to tell him about the evening's affair and their discovery of the melted coins, until breakfast the next morning. Fenton Hardy praised his sons, and advised them to work on the mystery along the lines they had adopted.

"Wish I could help you," he said, "but I start this morning on my trip in connection with that stolen gold I was telling you about. I'm taking the ten o'clock plane."

"Will Frank and I have to stay here with 'Mr Spanish'?" asked Joe. "We'd like to work on the melted coin case."

"I'll make arrangements to have a plain-clothes man come and stay here while I'm away," replied his father, just as Aunt Gertrude entered the room.

"What! Isn't it bad enough to have the house all cluttered up with a crazy man for a guest? Now you're going to bring a detective here to live. I won't stand for it! I'll leave."

"Now Gertrude, you don't mean that, I'm sure," said Mrs Hardy. " 'Mr Spanish' is no trouble, and as for the plain-clothes man, he will be here for your own protection."

"There's something mysterious about this whole business that I don't know about," grumbled Aunt Gertrude. "The boys are out at all hours of the night. Burglars get in here. A man without a memory eats and sleeps here. Why must I be kept in the dark?"

Frank decided that it would do no harm to let her in on part of the mystery at any rate. From his father he got the two coins that had been found in the Morton field.

"It all began with these, Aunt Gertrude," he said, handing them to her.

The woman took the objects and examined each

with grim interest. Then, to the utter astonishment of her nephews, she looked up and said:

"Well, as I live and breathe—a Pine Tree Shilling and a piece of Hog Money! Where in the world did you get these? They're very rare!"

"Why, Aunty!" exclaimed Frank. "How do you happen to know so much about old coins?"

Aunt Gertrude had spoken impulsively. For a moment she looked flustered. Then she glared at her nephews.

"Surely a body can have some secrets!" she said tartly.

Whereupon, in considerable confusion, she stalked from the room, muttering something they could not hear. Fenton Hardy raised his eyebrows inquiringly and glanced at his wife.

"Seems as if my sister knows a good deal more than we've given her credit for," smiled the detective.

Frank and Joe were thinking fast: first of the episode at the railway station when she told them about the counterfeit coins; now, of her revelation about Chet's pieces; and last of all, her reference to a secret.

"Aunt Gertrude accuses us of being mysterious," said Joe. "She's pretty mysterious herself. What do you suppose the secret is, Dad?"

His father shrugged his shoulders. "I have often thought my sister should have been a detective," he replied. "She certainly can keep things to herself, she reads character pretty well, and sometimes she hits the nail on the head by combining intuition with deduction."

"I wonder if she really does know something about coins and counterfeiters that we ought to find out from her," mused Frank.

"It would be a challenge to try," replied Mr Hardy with a smile.

· 18 ·

Counterfeits

"Boys," said Mrs Hardy a few minutes after her husband had left for the airport, "do you mind going over to Mawling for me again this morning? I have more club funds to deposit in the bank."

Frank and Joe smiled at their mother.

"Give us the money and we'll be off like a shot," added Joe.

Thus it happened that the brothers were in Mawling when Joe thought he saw old man Ratchy. While Frank went to the bank, Joe waited in the car, taking in the sights of the active little town.

Small though the village was, it had two banks, facing each other in the main square. Joe, glancing idly round, saw Ratchy descend the steps of the Peoples Bank. The bent figure disappeared around the corner of the building into the next street.

Instantly Joe jumped from the car and hurried across the square. When he rounded the corner of the Peoples Bank and looked up the side street, the elderly man was nowhere to be seen.

"I wonder if he *was* Ratchy. Maybe I can find out in the bank."

He went inside. There were no other customers there at the moment.

"An old man was in here a few minutes ago," Joe said to the teller. "Do you know his name?"

The man shook his head. "No, I don't. He came in to change some money."

"Dimes?" asked Joe.

The teller glanced at him in surprise.

"How did you know? Sure—he had a lot of dimes he wanted to change into notes. Several dollars' worth."

"Did he tell you the money was the proceeds from a children's entertainment?"

Again the teller looked surprised.

"You seem to know a good deal about the old fellow. What's the trouble? Anything wrong?"

"If the coins were counterfeit, you'd know, I suppose," said Joe.

"Counterfeit? I should say I *would* know. He couldn't get away with trying to pass any bogus silver on me."

The bank teller opened a roll of the coins. He examined several of them closely, tested the milled edges with his thumb, rang them on the counter.

"They're good all right. What's it all about? What made you think they might be counterfeit?"

"I didn't think they were counterfeit. But I just thought I'd make sure."

Leaving the man scratching his head in some bewilderment, the Hardy boy left the bank. He crossed the square just as Frank emerged from the other bank. Joe told his brother what had happened.

"It must have been Ratchy," agreed Frank. "I wish you had followed him."

"What I can't figure out is, if Ratchy is stealing old coins and is mixed up with counterfeiters, why would he go round changing good money at banks?" asked Joe, puzzled.

"I have an idea about that," said Frank. "Suppose the counterfeit coins were quarters and half dollars. He wouldn't try to pass them at a bank. He would go round to stores, making little simple purchases; a packet of chewing gum, or a newspaper, for instance. He'd get his change in small ones—good money in return for bad. Then he'd go to a bank whenever he had enough dimes to make it worthwhile. The dimes would be changed into notes."

Joe was sure his brother had hit upon the correct solution. He suggested that they investigate to see if Ratchy had obtained some of his coins in Mawling. A nearby store seemed to offer possibilities. They went in and asked an attendant if an old man had been there recently.

"Yes. There was one in here about half an hour ago. He bought a packet of envelopes."

"Did he get change for a quarter or half dollar?"

"I don't remember," said the girl. "Why?"

"Will you see if you have any coins that aren't authentic?" asked Frank.

She looked at the Hardys strangely, but opened the cash register and produced several coins. She examined them, then rang each one against the wood.

"Good as gold. Why do you ask?"

"We're looking for fake coins," said Frank.

The boys went from counter to counter, but found no bogus money. They left the store, puzzled. Perhaps Frank's theory had been wrong after all.

In quick succession they visited a shoe repair shop, a newsagents, and an ice cream shop. In each place they remembered the old man. He had made small purchases and received change for a quarter or half dollar. But the money was genuine.

Baffled, the brothers went into a café. It was near lunch time, and they were hungry. They ordered sandwiches, and while they waited, they tried to figure out what was wrong with the theory.

"Perhaps Ratchy really needed these things and he didn't wish to run the risk of passing any bad money in the town where he changes his coins at the bank," Joe suggested.

"That could be the answer," agreed Frank. "We may have to try to pick up his trail in some other town."

The sandwiches were ready. Frank paid for them and received change of a quarter. He looked at it intently, then nudged Joe.

"This is just like the counterfeits Aunt Gertrude got on the train," he whispered.

"What's that? Counterfeits?" asked the cafe owner, who had overheard the word.

Frank explained that the coin was bogus.

The man picked up the coin. "Hm, it sure *looks* good. But I guess it isn't." He shook his head in disgust. "Someone must have slipped it over on me. I wouldn't want you boys to think *I* was trying to do that, though."

He was full of apologies, and gave them good money. Frank and Joe were excited.

"Was an old man in here a little while ago?" the former asked eagerly.

The restaurant owner reflected. "Yes. Old fellow with a beard. He had breakfast. Say, do you think it was him that gave me that bad coin? Now that I think of it, he paid me with a half dollar and a quarter."

The man turned to the cash register and extracted a half dollar. It was a very cleverly made counterfeit. The victim fumed with anger.

"If I ever lay my hands on that old rascal, I'll have him thrown in jail," he declared.

"Maybe we can help you in that," said Frank.

"Please let us have the bad money to take with us."

The boys ate their sandwiches and hurriedly left the place. Since Mawling was not a large town, they hoped to pick up Ratchy's trail easily.

"Let's start at the bank and work in different directions," suggested Frank.

"All right. We'll meet here to report."

The brothers separated. For twenty minutes they inquired of various people but no one had noticed Ratchy.

After asking several more people if they had seen anyone answering the old man's description, they met a little girl in a street on the edge of town. She nodded emphatically in reply to their enquiry.

"I saw an old man like that," she said. "He came up from the bank just ahead of me."

"Did you notice which direction he went?"

"He didn't go in any direction. He walked into that house across the street."

The youngster pointed to a small, neglected-looking place set back in a weed-grown garden. Frank and Joe thanked the girl, and hurried over to the house, which seemed deserted. They went up to the door and knocked.

After a moment they heard footsteps. The door was opened by a burly individual of about thirty-five.

"What do you want?" he growled.

Then he frowned in sudden recognition. At the same moment Frank uttered a yell of astonishment. The man, untidily dressed, had his shirt open down the front, revealing an expanse of chest.

Upon that chest was tattooed the design of a Spanish woman's head!

·19·

The Fugitive

"It's the hold-up man?" cried Frank.

The fellow with the tattoo leaped back and slammed the door just as the youth sprang forward. The Hardy boys heard a key click in the lock, and footsteps thudding down the inner hall.

"I'll go round to the back!" shouted Joe.

He raced from the door. But there was no sign of the man. He tried the back door, but it was locked.

Suddenly the Hardys heard a heavy thud and a noise, as if someone had crashed into bushes. They ran to one side of the building just in time to see the tattooed man scrambling over a fence. The boys rushed after him, vaulting the fence. Then began a real chase which led farther and farther into the country. Athletic though the boys were, they began to get winded. They realized that their quarry was not only a husky individual, but desperate as well.

"He's—he's gone!" gasped Frank.

The tattooed man had vanished suddenly, although there were only open fields ahead. The pursuers raced forward, looking everywhere for him. In the middle of a pasture thick with weeds stood a weather-beaten, wooden box.

"Must be in there," declared Joe breathlessly.

Both boys pulled at the lid, which finally flew up.

At the same moment, the fellow they were after

leaped from the box. Joe tackled him by the legs. Frank flung an arm about the man's neck.

The fugitive struggled furiously, but the brothers clung to him grimly. Frank twisted his arms behind him until finally he yelled for mercy.

"I give up!" he shouted. "Let go of me!"

"How about that money you stole from me?" demanded Frank.

"I'll give it back. I promise. Let me up, and I'll give it to you."

The boys released him. Sullenly he dug into his pocket and produced a wad of notes.

"You'll find it all there," he growled.

"So far, so good," said Frank. "And now you'd better come along with us."

"You ain't going to turn me over to the police, are you?" whined the prisoner. "I've given you back your money. What more do you want?"

"You held me up, knocked me out, and left me in a ditch," Frank reminded him. "That's a police matter."

"Aw, don't do that, fellows," begged their captive. "You got your money back, didn't you? Do you want to see me sent to jail?"

"What's your name?" Frank asked the man.

"Butch Bauer. I'm a sailor," returned the other sullenly. "Leastways I used to be."

"How did you get that tattoo mark on your chest?"

"What do you want to know for?"

"I'll make a bargain with you," said Frank. "If you answer a few questions, I won't tell the police that you knocked me out. First, how did you get that tattoo?"

"I wish I'd never seen the thing," growled Butch Bauer. "I got it done in Mexico. I was in Vera Cruz and I ran into some old pirate who said he'd tattoo a picture of a beautiful girl on my chest. So this is what I got. And I've had bad luck ever since."

"Who did the tattooing?" asked Joe.

"I don't remember," grumbled Bauer. "Right after the job was done, I lost my money and missed my ship. From then on I've just had bad luck. Took to stealing. If you turn me over to the police now, it's all up with me. Give me a break, boys. I'm not a bad guy."

"Was the tattoo man a fellow called Blackbeard?"

Butch Bauer shook his head. "No. They called him Needles Ned."

"Did he have a black beard? Was there a fellow with him called Lopez?"

Bauer hesitated a moment, then said he thought the tattoo artist was red-haired.

"Ever heard of the *Curse of the Caribbees?*" asked Frank.

Bauer looked at the boy in surprise.

"I've heard of it okay. From Needles Ned himself."

"What did he say about it?" Joe asked excitedly.

"Nothing much, but it seemed to make him happy to get the design tattooed on me."

Frank and Joe glanced at each other. The same thought had occurred to the Hardys. Perhaps this clue from Bauer, slight thought it was, might be of help to "Mr Spanish".

"I think you'd better come along with us," said Frank to their prisoner.

"You're not turning me over to the police?" whined Butch Bauer.

"We want you to come home with us. A friend of ours is interested in the *Curse of the Caribbees*. We'd like you to tell him your story."

Butch Bauer was suspicious. But his objections to

going with the Hardys were quickly stilled when they threatened to turn him over to the police if he did not do so. Reluctantly, he accompanied them to Mawling and climbed into their car. Frank drove, while Joe took charge of the prisoner in the back seat.

On the way home they asked Bauer whether he lived in the house where they had seen him. He said he did not, but would not reveal who did, nor his own address.

"How about the old man? Does he live there?" asked Frank.

"Who do you mean?"

"Ratchy."

"Never heard of him."

"Maybe that isn't his right name," said Frank. "He's old and bent. Has a beard."

"Nobody like that was around there while I was in the house," replied Bauer. "Leastways I didn't see him: but then I wasn't there long."

The sailor would not say why he had come to the place, and remained silent for the rest of the journey.

When they reached the Hardy house, they saw "Mr Spanish" sitting on the lawn enjoying the late afternoon sunshine. As the boys came up the path with Bauer, they watched the men closely to see if there was any sign of recognition. But the two regarded each other impassively.

"You've never seen this man before?" Frank asked Bauer.

"Stranger to me," grunted the prisoner.

"This sailor knows something about the *Curse of the Caribbees*, 'Mr Spanish', " said Joe. "We thought he might be able to help bring back your memory. Go ahead and tell your story, Bauer."

The fellow repeated what he had already told the

boys, but apparently nothing in the tale stirred any chord of recollection for "Mr Spanish".

"I am most sorry," he said apologetically. "Vera Cruz—the tattoo man—the curse—it brings back nothing of my old life."

He got up from his chair and walked sadly into the house.

"Well, that didn't do much good," grunted Bauer. "How about letting me go now, huh?"

The boys were dubious, and just at that moment the plain-clothes man came out of the house.

"Mr Hardy said I might go out when you boys returned," he declared. "He says you——"

Just then the detective saw their prisoner.

"Why, it's Butch Bauer!" he roared gleefully.

The man lunged and tried to escape, but the plain-clothes man's big hand closed on his collar.

"We've been looking for this guy for months! Wanted for half-a-dozen hold-ups and burglaries.

He snapped handcuffs on his struggling captive.

"Where'd you find him, boys? Why, this fellow Bauer is one of the meanest thieves in the state."

The boys explained where they had picked up Bauer. They said little about his hold-up of Frank; only enough to let the plain-clothes man know why they had captured him.

"I guess I'd better search you," said the detective, going through the man's pockets.

He brought out various articles of little value. The Hardys looked on, not particularly interested until some coins were produced from the prisoner's trousers.

"Let me see those," said Frank excitedly.

When the boy inspected them, he was sure they were counterfeit. Bauer looked frightened but said nothing.

"Where'd you get these?" Frank asked him.

"I dunno. Some store, I guess."

The other did not believe him.

"We'll get it out of him at headquarters," said the plain-clothes man. "Come along, Bauer."

He dragged the protesting prisoner away.

"So he's a big crook after all," said Frank to his brother. "That hard-luck story was just a lot of bluff."

"Now I'm more convinced than ever there's some connection between him and Ratchy!" exploded Joe. "He just wouldn't tell us!"

The boys went indoors. Frank telephoned to Chief Collig, telling him about the coins and suggesting that the police in Mawling watch the house where they had found Butch Bauer.

Aunt Gertrude came into the hall a moment later carrying a tray. She looked a bit flustered when she saw her nephews.

" 'Mr Spanish' looked so peaked and tired when he came in, I thought I'd take him up a snack," she explained.

As she disappeared round the turn in the stairs, Frank winked at his brother.

"There," he said, "is the lady who wasn't going to stay in the same house with 'Mr Spanish'. "

The boys heard their aunt knock at the door of the guest room. Then came the sound of the door being opened.

A second later the brothers were startled to hear a loud exclamation from Aunt Gertrude. It was followed by a crash of dishes.

"Great Scot, what's happened?" yelled Joe.

"Perhaps 'Mr Spanish's' memory has returned!"

The Hardy boys rushed up the stairs.

20

Melted Coins

FRANK and Joe hurried into the guest room. 'Mr Spanish', looking very bewildered, was sitting in an armchair by the window, with Aunt Gertrude standing beside him in the scattered debris of broken dishes.

"Please give it to me!" she was begging. "It can't be of any value to you."

The man stared at her in perplexity. In the palm of his outstretched hand the boys saw the queer gold coin they had found in the secret pocket of his suit.

"I—I'm sorry," he said. "But I feel that I cannot part with this."

"What good is it to you? Why do you want to keep it? Please!"

Frank and Joe had never before seen Aunt Gertrude so pathetically anxious. She was like a child begging for a new toy. But "Mr Spanish" demurred. He closed his hand over the piece of money.

"It is all I have," he objected. "All I have from my past life."

Aunt Gertrude turned away, and began picking up the broken dishes.

"Oh, very well," she said. "Keep it if it's so precious to you. But I should think a man who is living with strangers——"

"Mr Spanish" flushed with embarrassment. He got up from his chair.

"If you mean this coin should be used to pay the expense of my food and lodging——"

"I didn't mean that," declared Aunt Gertrude, realizing she had spoken too hastily.

"I must leave here," said the man with dignity. "After all, it is not right that I should stay and be a burden to strangers. I shall go at once."

Frank stepped forward. "Please wait a minute, 'Mr Spanish', " he said. "You mustn't do that. In the first place, we're not strangers. At least, I hope you don't regard us that way."

"And in the second place, you didn't force yourself on us. We invited you here," added Joe. "Isn't that right, Aunt Gertrude?"

"Of course that's right," she agreed, eager to make amends for the trouble she had caused. "The man is talking perfect nonsense. We're delighted to have you here, 'Mr Spanish'. " She gathered up the last of the broken dishes. "Don't know what came over me," she muttered. "When I saw that coin——"

She piled the fragments on the tray and hurried from the room. Frank and Joe had to exert all their powers of persuasion to convince their guest that he should stay, but he finally agreed.

"You are all most kind," he smiled. "I should have known that none of you would make me feel unwelcome. I hope some day to be able to repay you. And now," he held out the coin, "if you will give this to the lady——"

"Oh, no," said Frank. "You may need that some day to help prove your identity."

They refused to accept the gold piece. Later, downstairs, they explained to Aunt Gertrude that the strange coin was the only clue they had towards helping them learn who "Mr Spanish" was. Frank told her that it had been hidden in a secret pocket of his suit, and therefore must be precious.

"Up to now we haven't been able to find out what the coin is," said Joe. "Apparently it's very rare."

"Why didn't you tell me this when you found it out?" demanded Aunt Gertrude. "That's what comes of keeping secrets from me. My goodness, I can probably solve this whole mystery for you myself."

"Do you mean you know something about 'Mr Spanish' and the gold coin?" gasped Frank.

"I know more than I'm telling," said his relative mysteriously, and refused to discuss the matter any further.

The next morning Fenton Hardy returned from his business trip. His sons could hardly wait to hear the outcome of his endeavours, and wondered if he had been successful in solving the mystery of the shipment of gold.

"As a matter of fact, I was partly successful," the detective told them as the three sat in the library soon after his return. "That suggestion of yours, Joe, was what really put me on the right track."

"What was that?" asked his son in surprise.

"You had an idea that the coins might have been melted down, so that's the lead I was following. I discovered that an old gold mine in the west coast had been bought cheaply by a group of men from the east, although everyone thought the mine had been worked out years ago. The surprising part of it was that they began shipping gold bars to the government soon after the purchase. They said they had struck a new vein of ore."

"And hadn't they?" asked Frank.

"No. The mine had been worked out. There wasn't any ore in it, and after a time it was abandoned. I discovered that the men were using the place as a blind."

They were receiving gold bars probably from the east, reshipping them from the mine to the government, and getting paid well for them."

"So that's the way the thieves disposed of the foreign gold?" Frank questioned his father.

"Yes. My theory is that some of the bars came from the gold coins that were in the shipment. They were melted down. The thieves probably figured out this method of getting rid of them without being caught."

"I wonder if they're the same crowd who are behind the counterfeit silver coins that have been circulating round here," Joe said.

"Maybe," returned his father, "but I'm inclined to think the local outfit works on a smaller scale. Possibly they're a cheaper gang of crooks who would steal anything. They may have taken over some of the equipment of the gold syndicate. At any rate, it is now my job to track down that equipment and the men who sold the gold to the government."

"Wasn't anyone at the mine when you got there?"

"No. The outfit had been gone some time. But I had a good chance to look round." Mr Hardy examined some notes he had made on his trip. "Frank," he said, "will you run upstairs and get me one of my old letter files from the attic? I had some special correspondence about gold a few years ago. It's a file marked 'G'. You'll find it on an old table at the head of the attic stairs."

His son was glad to be of service. He hurried to the second floor hall and started to open the door of the stairway leading to the attic.

It struck him as odd that the door was not tightly closed. Ordinarily no one would go into the attic for days at a time. Now Frank had a strong conviction that someone had just come down or had just gone up.

This was strange, as he thought his mother and Aunt Gertrude had left the house, and "Mr Spanish" was out walking with the plain-clothes man.

Quietly Frank examined the steps. They were slightly dusty, revealing footprints. They led all the way up the stairs. There were none leading down.

Was another burglar in the house? Whom would the boy meet if he should ascend?

Breathless with excitement, Frank walked up on tip-toe. A step creaked. In the attic he thought he heard a rustle. He stood motionless for a few moments, looking up. There was utter silence above.

He took another step. There was a second rustle. The boy was sure now that someone was in the attic.

Suddenly he heard the distinct clink of a coin, as if it had dropped against another piece of metal. Frank stole on up the stairs. When he reached the level of the attic floor, he raised his head cautiously.

There, not five feet from him, was Aunt Gertrude, kneeling on the floor beside an old trunk. Quite unaware of the presence of her nephew, she was thumbing the pages of a book.

For a moment Frank experienced keen disappointment. That the mysterious attic visitor should be no one more sinister than Aunt Gertrude was pretty much of a let-down. Then he saw something else, something so significant, that he uttered a gasp of astonishment.

On the floor beside the trunk was a great heap of coins!

The boy's involuntary gasp gave him away. Aunt Gertrude looked up in alarm. She opened her mouth and screamed.

"Frank Hardy, what do you mean by spying on me?" she cried out in dismay.

21

Aunt Gertrude's Hobby

AUNT GERTRUDE later claimed that Frank had frightened her out of seven years of her life. As it was, honours were about even, because her scream had startled the boy so thoroughly that he almost had tumbled down the stairs.

"My goodness, Aunty!" he spluttered. "It's only me!"

"Then you ought to be ashamed of yourself," snapped the woman, still trembling from the sudden shock of seeing Frank.

Frank was looking at the pile of coins on the floor. Aunt Gertrude flushed.

"You were spying on me!"

Her scream had aroused the rest of the household. First up the stairs was Joe. Next appeared Fenton Hardy. Finally came "Mr Spanish", asking if he could be of any help. He had just returned from his walk with the plain-clothes man, who had gone out again on an errand.

"Great Scot!" exclaimed Joe, when he spied the money on the floor. "Where did you find these, Aunt Gertrude?"

The woman gave in. She flung up her hands in a gesture of surrender.

"Oh, all right—all right," she said. "Now you know my secret. I suppose there'll be no peace in this house until I tell you all about it. I've been collecting coins for years, and keeping them in this trunk. I just came up here to have a quiet look at them, because I had an idea."

"Do you mean to say you collected all these, and never said a word about them, Gertrude?" asked Fenton Hardy astonished,. "I remember you had a small coin collection when you were a girl, but I didn't think you had kept up the hobby."

"This is what it has grown to be now," said his sister, indicating the imposing array of gold and silver coins on the floor. "It's my hobby. I've spent a great deal of money getting these pieces together. Too much, in fact. That's why I never said anything about them. I was afraid you'd think I was foolish."

"Not necessarily," said Mr Hardy kindly. "Your collection may be very valuable—a good investment. It's probably worth more now than what you spent on it."

"In that case it's worth a good deal of money," she answered. "There are some very fine specimens in this collection." Fondly she picked up one of the coins. "Here's a Queen Anne shilling of 1706, issued just before the Union of England and Scotland. And here's a hammered shilling issued in the reign of Queen Elizabeth of England. All my coins have woman's heads on them; I don't buy any others."

Frank and Joe now knew why their aunt had been so eager to obtain the coin "Mr Spanish" had. They wondered if perhaps she knew what it was, since she had a good knowledge of coins.

Aunt Gertrude picked up another specimen from the heap. "Here is the only United States piece with a ruler's head on it. Do you know who that was?" she asked.

The Hardy boys and the others shook their heads. "Another Queen," declared Aunt Gertrude. "Queen Isabella of Spain. During the Exposition in Chicago in 1893, in honour of Columbus, our Treasury issued forty thousand dollars' worth of coins in honour of Isabella of Spain. That's the only time a sovereign's head ever appeared on United States money."

Engrossed in talking about her hobby, Aunt Gertrude had scarcely noticed that "Mr Spanish" had drawn closer to the collection. Suddenly he dropped to his knees and began handling the gold and silver pieces. He deftly picked them up one by one, and examined both sides before setting them down again.

Frank nudged Joe in excitement. Then he nodded at his father.

It was apparent from "Mr Spanish's" dexterity that he was no novice in the handling of rare coins. He did it with the ease of long practice and familiarity, rubbing his thumb along the milled edges, holding the older and more deeply worn coins at the precise angle where they would catch the most light to reveal every detail of inscription or design.

"Do you remember any of them, 'Mr Spanish'? " asked Frank quietly.

The man glanced up in surprise, as if suddenly realizing where he was. The look of excitement and animation that had made his face glow with interest as he examined the money vanished. He shook his head.

"No—no," he said slowly. "I am sorry. They mean nothing. And yet when I saw them, I found myself wanting to look at them, to handle them. It is very strange. It is as if I know these coins. But I do not know them."

Aunt Gertrude glanced at him suspiciously.

"I have an odd Mexican piece here," she said. "It's a bit like the one you have downstairs." She fumbled through the collection and handed him the coin she had in mind. "Does that recall anything to you, 'Mr Spanish'? "

Their guest inspected the money carefully. But again there was no response. He shook his head.

"I'm sorry," he said, discouraged.

"One thing I will say," observed Mr Hardy to his sister. "As you know, there have been two thefts of coin collections in Bayport in the past few days. I hardly think it wise for you to leave such a valuable one as this in an old trunk in our attic."

"You're right, Fenton," declared Aunt Gertrude. "As a matter of fact, that is one reason why I came up here—to see if the money was still safe. I think I should keep it under lock and key. In a vault."

"In Bayport?" asked Joe.

"I have a deposit box in the bank at Hanover. That is where this collection is going. I'm taking no chances," declared Aunt Gertrude firmly. "Will you boys help me pack up the coins, and drive me over to the bank first thing in the morning?"

While Frank and Joe remained in the attic to help their aunt pack and sort the pieces, Fenton Hardy and "Mr Spanish" went downstairs. The detective asked his guest to let him see the gold coin again.

"If you don't mind," said Mr Hardy, taking paper and pencil from his pocket, "I'm going to make a tracing of this. It may be helpful."

When he had done this, he folded the paper and put it in an envelope.

"If it will help me learn who I am," said "Mr Spanish" seriously, "I shall owe much to this coin."

The detective did not tell his guest, but his sister had given him an idea. He would send the tracing with a letter to Mexico City. Possibly the strange piece could be identified by the authorities there.

Upstairs the two boys were working industriously. There was a good deal of detail involved in sorting out Aunt Gertrude's collection the way she wanted it. Furthermore, every time she picked up a coin she gave a brief account of its history and probable value. Each piece had to be recorded separately in a small book. Before the boys knew it, an hour had passed.

"Mother is calling us to dinner," said Joe.

"We've just about finished," replied Aunt Gertrude.

That night she slept with the valuable collection under her mattress for safe-keeping. The next morning she woke her nephews early, and shortly after nine o'clock they set out for Hanover in the car. Aunt Gertrude got into the rear seat with the collection, now securely wrapped in a box.

"Keep to the main road and don't dawdle," she ordered Frank, who took the wheel. "I don't want any more hold-ups. I won't draw an easy breath until my coins are safe."

They reached Hanover without incident. Aunt Gertrude directed them down a street which ran parallel with the railway track. There was a good bit of traffic, so Frank drove slowly, looking for a place to park.

Suddenly Joe cried out in excitement, "Wait a minute! Look, Frank! Down the street!"

From the bank, which was a hundred feet further on, emerged an old man who looked like Ratchy.

"Watch him, Frank!" said Joe. "I'm going to find out what he was doing in the bank."

He scrambled out of the car and ran up the steps.

"There's Ratchy!" cried Joe

At the same time Frank jumped out and took off in pursuit of Ratchy, who was crossing the street.

At the sight of the old man, the boys had forgotten everything regarding their original mission. Aunt Gertrude, fuming and muttering against boys in general, clutched the box of coins grimly, got out of the car, and marched quickly towards the bank alone.

"I never saw such boys," she grumbled.

In the meantime Joe had hurried up to a teller. Breathlessly he asked if an elderly customer had just changed a lot of dimes.

"Plenty of them. Nearly twenty dollars' worth. Why?"

"Did he say how he got them?"

"Children's entertainment. Admission charges, he told me."

"Thanks a lot," said Joe, and turned away.

"Wait!" called out the teller. "Explain what this is all about? Is there any reason why I shouldn't have changed the money?"

"Sorry—I'm in a hurry."

Joe strode towards the door, failing to see Aunt Gertrude, who was just entering the vault at the back of the bank. Several people looked at the excited boy in wonder.

When he got outside, his brother was not in sight. Neither was Ratchy.

"Wonder where they went?" he thought.

Deciding to ask Aunt Gertrude, Joe walked towards the car. Then he saw that she too had vanished.

While he was pondering what to do, the Hardy boy heard the noise of a train. One was pulling into the local station just across the street.

"I'll bet that's where Frank is," he decided. "Ratchy is going to take the train!"

Joe ran across the street and through the station entrance. Near the line stood Frank, looking up and down.

"All aboard!" shouted the guard.

"Didn't you see him?" Joe asked his brother, gasping for breath.

The last carriage passed by before the older boy answered the question.

"No old man got on the train," he reported. "Was the one in the bank Ratchy?"

"Yes. We mustn't let him get away. He can't be far off. We must find him!"

Frank did not move. He was still looking after the disappearing train.

"We've been tricked," he said at last. "No old man came out of this station, but one certainly came in. I know it."

"You mean he's hiding in this building?"

"No, he got on the train."

"But you said——"

"There's not a minute to lose! Follow me!" cried Frank, starting to run.

· 22 ·

On the Trail of Lopez

"WHERE are you going?" asked Joe, following his brother.

"I'm going to follow the train in the car," Frank replied. "We may be able to catch it at the next station."

"But why?"

"Ratchy certainly didn't take long to make his getaway," said Frank, as they ran. In fact for an old man, he was pretty quick. So I think he isn't an old man after all. He's a young fellow in disguise!"

This idea had not occurred to Joe. But when he thought it over, he agreed that his brother might very well be right. After all, old man Ratchy had disappeared quickly and completely. He could have gone into the station toilets and in a moment removed wig, beard and long coat and put them into the hold-all which he was carrying.

The brothers raced down the street towards the corner where they had parked the car. Aunt Gertrude was just returning to it.

"Well, I must say you boys left me in a hurry!" she snapped. "What was the idea of running away like that? I had to handle that safety box all by myself."

"We're in a hurry, Aunty," panted Joe. He helped her into the back seat, slammed the door, then scrambled into the front beside his brother. "We have to catch a train."

The car shot forward. Aunt Gertrude uttered a cry of dismayed protest.

"Now, wait a minute! What's this all about? I'm not going on any wild ride——"

The rest of her remarks were lost as the car zoomed along the road which ran parallel to the railway tracks, and Aunt Gertrude slid into the corner of the seat.

While she spluttered angrily, Joe explained the reason behind their hurried departure from Hanover. Finally, as Frank guided the car out on the open road, Aunt Gertrude began to appreciate the excitement of the chase.

"If that man is mixed up with counterfeiters, I'd like to get my hands on him too," she said with vehemence. "I haven't forgotten how I was robbed!"

The next station was five miles away, but they overtook the train. It was just pulling in as the car skidded to a stop beside the entrance.

"Pick me up at the next station. I'll walk through the train," said Frank as he leaped from behind the wheel.

He crossed the platform at a run and swung himself aboard the last carriage. Joe reversed the car, and turned round to the main road. He passed the train about half a mile down the road, and pulled ahead of it. The next station was eight miles distant, and he reached it a few minutes before the train came into sight. When it pulled to a stop, Frank descended from the first carriage. He was alone. From the glum expression on his face it was obvious that he hadn't located Ratchy.

"No luck?" asked Joe.

Frank shook his head. "He may have been one of the young men aboard, but I couldn't identify any of them as Ratchy. I went through every coach. Not a person had a hold-all anything like the one I saw the old fellow carrying."

Aunt Gertrude sniffed.

"Now that this wild-goose chase is over," she said, "perhaps you'll be good enough to take me home."

Chastened, the boys drove their aunt to Bayport. When they reached the house, their mother told them Chet Morton had telephoned a few minutes before.

"He seemed very excited," she said. "I promised you'd get in touch with him as soon as you came in."

When Frank called Chet, the fat boy was in such a state of elation that he could hardly speak.

"C-c-come out here r-r-r-right away," he stammered. "I've got big news. Run all the way. Oh, boy! Just wait till you see!"

Chet hung up the receiver.

"Sounds as if he's discovered a gold mine," said Joe when his brother relayed the conversation. "Let's go out there right away and see what happened."

Mrs Hardy insisted that the boys have lunch first, so it was after two o'clock before Frank and Joe reached the Morton farm. There they found Chet alone. He was in the back garden, just finishing a plate of doughnuts. He was pop-eyed with excitement.

"I found it all by myself!" he declared proudly, leading them into the house. "Saw a place that looked as if some fresh digging had been going on there, so I grabbed a shovel and went to work. Look!"

On the kitchen table stood a box. Inside this were scores of gold coins.

"The treasure!" declared Chet, slapping himself on the chest, and awaiting the congratulations of his friends.

Frank and Joe examined the coins. In the bottom of the box they found some numbered cardboard tickets, upon which were written descriptions of the pieces.

Frank looked at the back of one of these closely. There were two tell-tale words:

Carter Collection

He glanced up at Chet. "You've certainly made a find. But I'm sorry to tell you it isn't the treasure you were looking for."

"What do you mean? Don't you call that a treasure?"

"In a way—yes. But really it's a coin collection—the one that was stolen from Mr Carter's house in Bayport this week."

Chet was crestfallen. He had been so sure he had stumbled on the old treasure buried on the Morton farm that for a while he walked round the kitchen talking to himself ruefully. Finally he brightened up.

"Well, it's something to have found Mr Carter's collection anyhow. I guess he'll be mighty glad to get it back. You fellows had better return it to him. After all, you were working on the case."

"Suppose you come along with us. *You* found the collection," put in Frank.

"Not me," said Chet. "I'm going back to digging. I'll find that buried treasure if I have to spend the rest of my life with a shovel!"

The Hardys smiled. This was the first time in Chet's life they had ever known him to be looking for work.

"Where'd you find the coins?" asked Joe.

His chum grinned. "I was following Frank's route he drew on that map, just to help you fellows out. About five hundred feet beyond that old pit where I fell in, I saw the newly-dug spot I told you about."

"You're a real help, Chet," said Frank. "It proves

to me more than ever that the thief or thieves we're trying to locate head from Bayport in a westerly direction to their hideout. I mean to find that place one of these days!"

The Hardy boys decided to return Mr Carter's precious coins at once. The numismatist almost wept for joy when he saw his collection. He would have rewarded the boys on the spot, but they insisted that Chet deserved all the credit.

"In that case I'll see that he doesn't regret it," declared Mr Carter. "I'll send him a cheque. That collection is worth more to me than I can tell you. But isn't it strange that the thief buried it in a field?"

The boys did not mention their suspicions on this score, but after they left the house, they freely discussed this aspect of the case. Joe's theory was that the thief or thieves had hidden the coins in the field, with the idea of melting them down later to make counterfeits.

"Why do you suppose they didn't use the old pit?" said Joe. "Because they knew that it had been discovered?"

"I think not," replied Frank slowly. "In that case, they wouldn't have hidden the Carter coins near the Morton property at all. No, I believe that the man who hid the melted coins in the pit was double-crossing his companions."

"You mean he never turned them over to the other thieves, and planned to go back for them later and sell them or melt them on his own account?"

Frank nodded. "And I believe that person was Ratchy." Then a new thought struck him. "By the way, we ought to tell the police that Mr Carter's collection has been found. He is so overjoyed, it probably won't occur to him to do it."

He stepped into a telephone kiosk in a nearby shop. As the boy had suspected, the police had not been told about the return of the coins.

"That's fine," said Chief Collig to Frank when he heard the news. "Maybe I'd better send some of my men out to those fields past the Mortons to do some digging. We may find the Wakefield collection, too."

"I believe Chet will locate it if it is there," Frank replied.

Just then Joe, who was looking out of the shop window while his brother was telephoning, excitedly opened the door of the booth and touched Frank's shoulder.

"Quick, Frank—look!" he whispered. "Lopez!"

He gestured frantically towards a man who was crossing the street, hat pulled down low over his forehead. Then the Hardy boy dashed from the shop.

"Chief Collig!" said Frank urgently into the telephone. "I must go now. We've just seen Lopez. Can you get some men down here right away? We'll try to shadow him. I'm in a shop kiosk at the corner of State and Carteret Streets. Try to pick up our trail from here."

"All right, boy. Don't lose him. I'll send a patrol car out," promised the chief.

Frank ran from the kiosk.

"Watch which way we go and tell the police when they come," he cried to the astonished shop girl as he rushed out the door.

Frank overtook Joe in the next street. Lopez was about fifty yards ahead, walking rapidly. He darted into an alley, crossed over into another street, threaded his way through a number of lanes and byways, and headed towards the dock area.

"Perhaps he's seen us and is trying to shake us off," Joe suggested.

"Let him try." Frank had already spoken to several people. Now he stopped for a moment at a fruit stand. "Do us a favour, please?" he said to the proprietor. "Watch us until we're out of sight. The police may be along in a few minutes. Tell them which way we went."

The man blinked. When the Hardys looked back as they turned the next corner, the fruit seller was still peering after them in perplexity.

In this way, by speaking to one person after another, they tried to leave a trail as to the direction they took. But in the end, there was no one to whom they could give a final clue. In trying to find a person, the Hardys almost lost sight of Lopez. He seemed to vanish into thin air a moment after hurrying into a dark, narrow street. Joe spied him going up a stairway leading from the pavement.

"There he is! Come on!"

The brothers walked quietly up the steps. At the top a door stood half open. Frank advanced towards it and looked into the room beyond. There was a deep evil-sounding chuckle.

"Come in, boys! I was expecting you."

At the same moment a figure lunged at them from the shadows of the hall. Each of the Hardys was given a violent push. They stumbled forward into the gloomy room. As the door slammed behind them, the chuckle became an uproarious laugh.

"Yes, sir, I was expecting you. And here you are. The two of you!"

Lounging against the wall, his arms folded, was the sinister figure of Blackbeard in his full pirate's outfit. When the boys turned to see who had thrust them into the room they saw Lopez, smiling evilly, his back against the locked door!

"Ho-ho, so you're afraid now?" laughed Blackbeard sardonically. "Thought you were clever, following Lopez here. And him knowing you were behind him every foot of the way. 'Go out and bring them boys here,' I told him. 'Just go out in the streets and make sure they see you. They'll follow. Lead 'em here,' I said. Didn't I, Lopez?"

The servant bowed. Blackbeard burst into a wild bellow of laughter. The Hardys were crestfallen.

"Aye, lads," roared the pirate, "it's the sort of trick my ancestor Blackbeard himself would have enjoyed."

He rose, picked up a small carved chest from a table, brought it before his captives, and opened the lid. Frank and Joe got a strong whiff of a sweet, sickening incense.

"Just to make you peaceful," said the pirate, closing the lid.

Fearing they would be overcome by the strange odour, the brothers dodged to the other side of the room. What would this fiend attempt next?

"I have a story to tell you," Blackbeard grinned. "But first you must be in the proper mood. Don't try to get away, my lads."

He followed them, carrying the chest. The boys wondered if they should tackle the two men before they had a chance to execute some dire plan. Frank and Joe realized they might be tattooed with the *Curse of the Caribbees*, or become the victims of some other awful scheme of these pirates.

"Let's fight 'em!" Joe urged his brother.

But neither he nor Frank had the power to do so. Suddenly their muscles seemed to become paralysed. Slowly they sank to the floor.

The Pirate's Clue

LOPEZ propped the Hardy boys against the wall. They had never felt so odd before in their lives; their minds functioning normally, their bodies useless.

"I've got a story to tell you," roared Blackbeard, "before I tattoo you."

He straddled a chair resting his arms on the back.

"It's about coins!" he said abruptly. "It's come to my ears that you're interested in 'em."

The pirate smoothed his beard and went on.

"There was a fortune stolen once," he rumbled, "from a rich family in Mexico. I know, 'cause the tale came to me from a dying sailor. He had it straight from one of them that stole the money. Hid it in a cave, the bandits did—a cave guarded by snakes."

Blackbeard pointed a finger at his unwilling listeners.

"Bad luck came to every man who had anything to do with that stolen fortune," he said. "One by one, the bandits died. The man who told me where it was hidden came to a bad end. I took a few of the coins myself, and I've lived to regret it. On account of the curse put on the money, you see!"

"What curse?" asked Frank.

"Why, the *Curse of the Caribbees*, of course," roared Blackbeard. "The bandits didn't know about that, or they'd never have stolen the gold pieces. It was put on all thieves who might steal any of 'em. I guess it was true, 'cause it fell on me. But I tried to avoid it by a charm."

Blackbeard rolled up one sleeve and extended his bared arm, revealing the design of a coiled snake.

"'Twas said you could guard against that Caribbee curse by tattooin' on this design before goin' to the cave for some of the coins. But it didn't do no good."

The pirate shook his head sadly. He reached into a pocket and took out a gold piece.

"There you are, lads! One of the coins that's responsible for the *Curse of the Caribbees*."

By this time Frank and Joe had come to the conclusion that Blackbeard was mad, but they forgot this when they looked at the coin in his hand.

"It's the same as 'Mr. Spanish's' gold piece," said Frank in amazement.

How he wished he could get it. Here was a wonderful clue, yet he was helpless.

"I also heard," grinned Blackbeard, "that you could get rid o' the bad luck by tattooin' this design on somebody else. And that's what I aim to do right now! You won't get away a second time!"

At that moment there was a thunder of footsteps on the stairs. Blackbeard leaped backwards.

"Lopez!" he roared. "Bar the doors! Block the windows! They're after me! 'Tis the *Curse of the Caribbees!*"

There was a resounding crash against the door. Another crash, and the panels splintered. Chief Collig and his men stormed into the room. Quickly they overpowered the struggling Blackbeard and Lopez.

"But you can't do this to me! I'm a descendant of Blackbeard, the most fearful pirate that ever sailed the Spanish Main!" roared the bearded prisoner. "I'll put the *Curse of the Caribbees* on you!"

"You watch your language and don't start any cursin' around here, or you'll be in more trouble," Collig warned him. "Go along quietly. Your sailing days are over, Mr Pirate."

It was not until the uproar had ended that the police realized Frank and Joe could not get up. Collig was fearful of their condition, and took the Hardys home himself. Before they reached the house, the brothers fortunately were all right again. The effect of the strange-smelling incense had worn off completely.

"We'll come down later to headquarters to talk to that tattoo pirate," said Frank, as the police car dropped them off.

As soon as they entered the house, the boys sought out their father in his study, and told him of their recent experience.

"Blackbeard claims he knows where a fortune in coins is buried. They're exactly like the one 'Mr. Spanish' has," said Frank excitedly. "Do you think we ought to get the two men together?"

Mr Hardy was thoughtful a moment. "Did Blackbeard tell you what the coin was?"

"We didn't have time to ask him."

The detective telephoned police headquarters and waited until the prisoner had been questioned. The report came back that the man did not know what the strange gold piece was. Mr Hardy hung up and turned to his sons.

"I ought to hear from Mexico City any time," he said. "It would be best to do nothing more until I get word."

He explained how he had made a tracing of "Mr Spanish's" coin, and sent it by air mail to Mexico. Half an hour later a reply came.

"This is a very interesting telegram," he said. "The Mexican authorities have identified my tracing. They say that a large sum of money in commemorative coins like 'Mr Spanish's' were struck in 1725 for the Arezo family of Carabaya."

"Carabaya?" repeated Joe. "Maybe it isn't the *Curse of the Caribbees* at all, but the curse of Carabaya!"

Frank was already turning the pages of an atlas. "Here it is. Carabaya," he said excitedly.

"We're really getting somewhere on this mystery now," said Joe. "Do you suppose 'Mr Spanish's' real name could be Arezo? I'm going to ask him."

"Not so fast, son," his father warned the boy. "Remember that two sinister characters, Butch Bauer and Blackbeard, both had something to do with the likeness of the strange Spanish woman's head, which by the way is called Doña Luisa. I'll call the State Department in Washington, and see if they have a record of any member of the Arezo family visiting this country."

In a few minutes he was speaking to a government official. The boys waited attentively until their father hung up. He smiled as he turned to his sons.

"The present head of the Arezo family is Ferdinand Arezo, *and he is now visiting in the United States!*"

" 'Mr Spanish?' " exclaimed Frank.

"Perhaps. I understand Señor Arezo is about thirty-five years old. When he came to this country, he was accompanied by a servant named Manuel and a small dog called Chico."

"And has this Señor Arezo disappeared?"

"My informant in Washington didn't know. For all he was aware, Señor Arezo has been on a tour of the country. But if he disappeared, it might be some time before inquiries would be started about him."

Again Joe mentioned taking this information to "Mr Spanish" at once. But Mr Hardy pointed out that he was afraid little or nothing would be gained by this method. If their guest could not remember his past, the mere mention of the name Arezo would hardly be likely to strike a responsive chord in his memory.

"I'd like to try another plan," he said. "Slip upstairs, Joe, and find out if 'Mr Spanish' is asleep. If he is, don't waken him."

The boy went upstairs quietly and returned to report their visitor was asleep.

"Good," smiled the detective. "Sometimes the sub-conscious mind will respond to impressions where the conscious mind will not. After all, 'Mr Spanish' hasn't exactly *lost* his memory. No one ever does. He has merely lost the key, the associations that will awaken his memory. I think we'll go upstairs and pay him a visit."

Fenton Hardy explained his plan. It was very simple —so simple that at first the boys doubted that it would work. But at least it was worth trying.

Quietly they stole into the guest room. The curtains were drawn. "Mr Spanish" was sleeping soundly.

The detective walked softly to the bedside. He leaned forward and spoke quietly:

"*Buenos dias, Señor Arezo!*"

"Mr Spanish" stirred, but did not open his eyes. At a signal Joe made sounds like the short, shrill barking of a small dog.

"No, no, Chico!" said Mr Hardy sternly.

Then Frank called out, "Manuel! Manuel!"

"Mr Spanish" stirred restlessly. Fenton Hardy signalled to his sons, and they left the room as quietly as they had entered it.

·24·

A Strange Story

THE Hardy boys and their father waited just outside the door of the guest room. There, at some distance from the bed, they repeated their performance.

"Manuel!" called Frank.

Joe barked frantically.

"Down, Chico! Down!" ordered Fenton Hardy. "I must go to Señor Arezo."

Frank peeped into the room. "Mr Spanish" was awake. He was sitting up in bed, staring straight before him with a strange, fixed expression on his face. The boy walked into the room.

"Good afternoon, Señor Arezo," he said.

"Good afternoon," returned the man with a puzzled frown. "Where is Manuel? Send him to me at once."

"I am sorry," replied Frank. "But Manuel is not here."

"Not here? But that is impossible. Manuel is always—" Then the Hardy's guest broke off in dismay as he looked about him. "Where am I? This room is strange to me. Who are you?"

"Don't you remember me? I'm Frank Hardy!"

Now it was the boy's turn to be astonished, because the man shook his head.

"I have never seen you before. Please explain this. Who are you and why am I here?"

Mr Hardy and Joe came in quickly.

"It's all right, Señor Arezo," said the detective, smiling. "You are Señor Arezo, aren't you?"

"But of course. Ferdinand Arezo."

"You met with an accident," explained Fenton Hardy. "You have been very ill. But I assure you that you are with friends. We've been doing our best to look after you."

Señor Arezo put his hands before his eyes.

"Ah, yes," he said. "I was walking down the street. A man came up and spoke to me. Suddenly he struck me and I remembered no more."

"That was several days ago," Frank told him. "Can you recall where you were and where you were going?"

"In the city of—Bayport, yes, Bayport," said Arezo. "I remember quite clearly. I was on my way to see a famous detective. His name—Hardy. Fenton Hardy. Of course I remember. Why shouldn't I?"

"Because," said Mr Hardy, "ever since the moment you regained consciousness several days ago, you have been unable to recall anything about your past life. It wasn't until we found a clue to your identity that we were able to arouse your memory at all."

Just then Aunt Gertrude came storming in.

"Now what is going on here?" she demanded. "What is the idea of disturbing 'Mr Spanish' when he's having his afternoon nap?"

"And who is this lady?" inquired Señor Arezo mildly.

Miss Hardy's mouth opened in astonishment.

"Well, I never!" she exclaimed. "Is this a game? Who am I supposed to be? Mother Hubbard?"

"How do you do, Señora Hubbard," said Arezo politely.

"Now wait a minute," snapped Aunt Gertrude. "I'm in no mood for this sort of nonsense."

Frank and Joe were snickering quietly, enjoying the mutual bewilderment of Señor Arezo and their aunt. Fenton Hardy turned to his sister.

"He isn't joking, Gertrude. He doesn't remember you, or any of us, as a matter of fact. May I present Señor Ferdinand Arezo, of Carabaya, Mexico, who has just recovered his memory?"

Aunt Gertrude took some time to digest this statement. She still was unsure that a joke was not being played upon her.

"Recovered his memory!" she snorted. "If you ask me, I think he's lost it worse than ever."

With further explanations, however, the woman was soon mollified and decided not to be offended by the fact that Señor Arezo could not remember her. The man got dressed and came downstairs, where the family gathered in the living-room to hear his story.

"I cannot tell you how grateful I am for your kindness," he said. "It is so strange that I should find myself in the very home to which I was going when I was attacked."

The Hardys explained how this had happened.

"Perhaps you will tell us why you were coming here," suggested Frank. "Did your visit have something to do with the Doña Luisa coins?"

"Ah, you know of them? Yes, it was about the coins. You see, the pieces were struck in honour of my ancestor, Doña Luisa, over two hundred years ago. They were never used outside of Carabaya until her grandson, then an old man, set out with a great many of them for the coast. He intended to spend the rest of his life in Spain, but was killed in the hills of Mexico by bandits who stole his money. Only a few of the coins ever turned up, because there was said to be a curse on them—the *Curse of Carabaya*."

"My brother guessed that," said Joe. "We heard it called the *Curse of the Caribbees*."

"Many people called it that, after a time, but it was the *Curse of Carabaya*. My father felt it was a disgrace to our family that the name of Arezo should be connected with such a story. He spent much time collecting any of the Doña Luisa coins he could get, but the bulk of them never turned up. When he was dying, he asked me to continue the work.

"I thought that some of the pieces might have fallen into the hands of collectors, so I used to carry rare coins with me. They helped as introductions to collectors, so that I could persuade them to sell me any Doña Luisa coins they might have."

"Was that the reason for your visit to this country?" asked Mrs Hardy.

"Yes, indeed. But I had not been here very long, when I was robbed of my coins. I sent Manuel and Chico back to Mexico and came on here to Bayport to consult with Mr Hardy about this."

"Why didn't you report your loss to the police as soon as it happened?" asked the detective.

"It was a delicate subject. I still had some Doña Luisa coins with me, and I was afraid of ridicule if the matter of the *Curse of Carabaya* should appear in the newspapers and get back to Mexico. I was told that there were no better detectives than Hardy and Sons," smiled Señor Arezo, "so I came here. But on my way to your house I was attacked and robbed of everything I had with me. Beyond that I remember nothing."

"Perhaps you'll really think Hardy and Sons are

good detectives," said Joe, "if we can put you on the track of most of the other Doña Luisa coins. Let's get the car out of the garage, Dad, and take Señor Arezo down to see Blackbeard."

"But this is amazing," said their guest, as he stepped into the car a few minutes later. "I do not understand. This Blackbeard—who is he?"

"He's a bit crazy—thinks he's a descendant of a pirate," explained Frank, "but I believe he may know where those bandits hid the Arezo money. Blackbeard is down at police headquarters."

When the car pulled up in front of the building, Mr Hardy, Joe and the Mexican got out. But Frank remained behind the wheel.

"Aren't you coming in with us?" asked his father.

"I've just had a hunch about finding the coins that were stolen from 'Mr Sp'—Señor Arezo," his son replied. "And also those melted coins. Do you mind if I take the car for a little while?"

"Go ahead," said Mr Hardy. "Have Joe go with you. After Señor Arezo and I talk to Blackbeard, we'll walk home."

Joe climbed back in and looked at his brother. "What's your hunch?"

Frank pulled a road map from his pocket. On it was the pencil line running from Bayport through the Morton farm to Hixon.

"This may be another wild-goose chase," he said, "but I don't think so. Look at these towns on the map." He pointed to Bayport, Mawling, Hanover. "What do you make of their locations?"

"Not much," confessed Joe. "Let's see. We caught Butch Bauer outside Mawling, heading towards Hanover. Ratchy was in Hanover and took a train."

"Exactly," said Frank gleefully. "If you draw a line from Mawling through Hanover, and follow the direction of Ratchy's train, you come to Tryton."

"Why stop there?"

"Because if you continue the other line from Bayport through the Morton farm and Hixon, you hit Tryton also."

"Gosh, that's clever, Frank," his brother praised him. "Well, what are we waiting for? Let's go to Tryton and find those men who stole the coins!"

"And melted them," said Frank.

"And made counterfeits out of them!" added his brother.

Frank drove as fast as he dared to the village they wanted to investigate. It was spread out over a large area, and included Upper Tryton, Lower Tryton, New Tryton, and Tryton Hills.

"I couldn't imagine a safer place for counterfeiters to hide," grumbled Joe, after the boys had ridden up one street and down another for half an hour. "What say we stop for a few minutes and get an iced drink? I'm terribly thirsty."

"Make it ice cream cones and I'll wait in the car," said Frank. "I may pick up a clue while you're in the café."

Joe disappeared inside, while his brother looked intently at each passer-by. Presently a car came along from the opposite direction and parked up the street, some yards away from the Hardy boys.

Frank eyed the driver as he got out and went into the post office. He was an old man. At this moment Joe returned, holding two ice cream cones.

"What's the matter?" he asked, when Frank paid no attention to him.

"That car by the post office. An old man got out of it and went into the place."

"Who was he? Not——"

"I merely got a glimpse of him. We'll watch and see if he's Ratchy."

At that moment the old man came out of the post office. He headed straight for the car parked at the kerb, and settled himself behind the wheel. The boys waited expectantly, hoping that at last they were going to catch one of the counterfeiters.

"He's coming this way! If it's Ratchy, we'd better duck, so he won't see us," advised Joe. "We don't want to lose him again."

The boy put his head down on the seat, but Frank merely covered his face with one hand to hide his identity. He got a good look at the suspect and almost yelled in astonishment and delight.

"A *young* man was at the wheel!" he said to Joe, as the car passed them. "Ratchy *does* use a disguise! Now I'm sure of it!"

" He certainly gets it on and off fast, but he won't run away this time. Why do you suppose he changed so suddenly?"

"May have been tipped off by a pal that you and I are here," guessed Frank.

Already he had started the engine. Now he pulled away from the kerb quickly and turned round. Then he shot off in pursuit of young Mr Ratchy!

The Capture

"AT THE rate Ratchy is driving, we're going to have a job keeping him in sight," said Joe to his brother.

Instead of trying to overtake Ratchy, Frank deliberately slowed down and allowed a big truck to get ahead of him. The vehicle screened the boys from view, but occasionally Frank would pull over to the middle of the road to make sure the suspect's car was still in front.

By this time they were on the outskirts of Tryton, driving towards open country. Fortunately, the heavy truck also was headed out of town. It followed the other car almost as if the driver were shadowing him too.

"I hope Ratchy doesn't see us," Joe said. "He'd change any plans he has in mind if he thinks we're closing in on him."

The man drove along at forty miles an hour down the main road. Finally he swung into a side road. A cloud of dust marked his course.

The truck rolled on without turning. Frank steered the Hardy car into the side road.

"Now Ratchy will see us," said Joe anxiously.

"Perhaps not," replied his brother. "The dust from his car may screen us."

The dust rose in a thick, billowy cloud. If Ratchy should look in his rear-view mirror, it was scarcely likely that he would see the car following him.

"Where do you suppose he is headed?" asked Joe.

"Tryton Hills, I think," said Frank. "This road doubles back there."

It dipped and wound among uplands and valleys. At last Tryton Hills came in sight. Anxiously the boys watched the hovering cloud of dust. At the village it began to settle.

Ratchy's car was not in sight!

In alarm the Hardys rode along the main street. Joe glanced up each side road. Finally, at the edge of town he excitedly asked Frank to stop.

"There's the car!" he cried. "Parked in front of an old house way back from the street. Let's go!"

"We'd better notify the police first," said his brother.

Frank drove past the corner and pulled in at the pavement. The boys got out, and called the local police from a telephone kiosk.

"We can't wait for them, though," said Frank, after Joe had hung up. "We'd better go right to the house."

The man's car still stood in front of the house.

"Take the back door. I'll go to the front one," said Frank as they hurried up the path.

Joe slipped round to the back of the house. As he ducked past a window, he noticed that it was boarded up. But he could hear voices inside.

Frank went to the front door and knocked sharply. He heard footsteps beyond. A voice said:

"Who's there?"

Frank spoke gruffly. "Lemme in, Ratchy—quick! Hurry up!"

A key grated in the lock. The door opened suddenly. The young man whom they had followed peered out. His eyes widened in alarm.

"Oh, no, you don't!" he snapped, and hastily tried to slam the door.

But Frank had thrust his foot over the threshold. At the same instant he lunged inside.

"Run, you guys!" yelled Ratchy. "It's the Hardy boys!"

Frank tackled the fellow. From the other rooms of the house he heard shouts and the thud of running feet. There was a yell of fright as one of the men evidently bumped into Joe at the back door.

Frank and Ratchy wrestled fiercely in the front hall. But the struggle was brief. As the man thrashed about wildly in his efforts to escape, there came the screech of brakes.

A car ground to a halt in front of the house. Out jumped four policemen. They raced up the path and plunged through the open doorway. At Frank's signal one of them pounced on Ratchy.

The police completed their round-up quickly. Four suspects were overpowered. One of them, who had managed to get away from Joe, was captured after a sprint across the back garden.

"I tell you I'm not mixed up in this. I'm not a counterfeiter," he whined. "I just came here to deliver a parcel."

"Who said you *were* a counterfeiter?" demanded the officer. Then he yelled, "Glory be—have we rounded up a gang of counterfeiters?"

Much to his astonishment, this proved to be the case. In the basement of the house was found a complete set of equipment for melting metal and stamping out quarters and half dollars. The Hardys also located a large quantity of coins that had not yet reached the melting pot, including Doctor Wakefield's collection.

"Well, Ratchy—if that's your name," said Frank, "it looks as if your little money-making business is broken up."

"You haven't got anything on me," the man growled. "I didn't do any counterfeiting."

"Maybe not. But you got rid of the bad money. Also, you stole collections. And how about the melted coins you took from here and hid in the old pit near the Morton farm?"

The last remark was a shot in the dark, but it told. Ratchy turned pale.

"I don't know anything about an old pit," he said feebly.

"What's this?" shouted one of the crew—a burly, red-haired man. He wheeled on Ratchy. "So that's what you've been up to? Double-crossing us, hey? Pretending you were hiding only the coin collections, and all the time stealing the melted coins from us and putting them away for yourself."

"Double-crosser!" shouted another one of them angrily. "You've probably been working on the side with the Cawdry gang, you rat. You've been helping those gold guys that sold us the melting equipment."

"You talk too much!" shouted Ratchy. "And so does Butch Bauer. If he hadn't squealed, we wouldn't have been caught!"

The Hardys smiled, for Bauer had confessed nothing. As the counterfeiter lunged at his pal in anger, the policemen took firmer grips on their prisoners.

"All right, break it up!" ordered the sergeant in charge. "We'll hear all about this later. You fellows can do your talking at headquarters."

At the police station the whole story came out. Ratchy, disguised as an old man, went from bank to bank, telling the false yarn about the admission money from the children's entertainments. Actually he had received them in change when passing worthless quarters and half dollars on unsuspecting people.

His other work was stealing coin collections, which could be melted down for the sake of the metal, and hiding them somewhere for a short time. Two of the other prisoners, who operated the counterfeiting equipment, occasionally went along to assist him. With the aid of a dog or two, they helped to create a diversion, so that Ratchy could enter a house undetected.

He also confessed that he had become frightened at the Bayport railway station when Aunt Gertrude had threatened to turn the counterfeit coins over to Mr Hardy. Using the disguise of a middle-aged man, Ratchy and his pals had tried to locate the tell-tale pieces at the detective's home, but had failed.

One of the hideouts of the gang was the house in Mawling where Bauer had been caught. The ex-sailor was a born thief, and went off on little excursions of his own to obtain additional cash for himself. Once, when Ratchy had sent him to spy on the Hardy home, he had overheard the story of the club money and robbed Frank of it. In his haste to get away, he had failed to find Chet's coins.

Frank asked Ratchy about the old pit near the Morton farm. "Did you build the platform in it?"

"Yes. I knew about the pit. Butch told me a story of how pirates built pits with platforms, so I thought I'd try one. You guys are smart all right. You nearly caught me that night I knocked your friend out."

"You did a good job on him," said Frank.

"Did you forget where you'd buried the melted coins?" asked Joe.

Ratchy admitted that he had been confused in the darkness. He insisted he had found nothing in Chet's ditch.

At that moment Fenton Hardy and Señor Arezo arrived. They had been summoned hastily from Bayport. The Mexican joyfully identified a bag of coins salvaged from the basement of the old house as his stolen collection.

But most interesting of all to Fenton Hardy was the clue about the Cawdry gang. When his sons told him about the slip one of the local counterfeiters had made, the detective asked Ratchy where the members of that group were.

"I'll tell you where Cawdry is right now," growled the prisoner vengefully. "It's not going to help me to protect those big shots any longer. They've been blackmailing me ever since I bought this outfit."

"That was the bunch who operated the abandoned gold mine out west," Mr Hardy explained later to the boys. "The last clue I needed to solve the mystery of the shipment of gold that disappeared from Bayport."

The next morning at breakfast, in response to messages he had sent to a large city in a nearby state, a telephone call came for Fenton Hardy. The Cawdry gang had been rounded up.

"A mighty fine piece of work you boys have done," he smiled at his sons, after he had come back to the table with the good news. "You get the credit for unearthing the information that turned the trick."

"A fine piece of work, too, which you all did for me," said Señor Arezo. "I shall be grateful always. Tomorrow I shall leave for Mexico with Blackbeard. The police have agreed to that. The man has promised to lead me to the cave where the Doña Luisa coins are hidden."

"I hope it'll be safe," sniffed Aunt Gertrude. "I thought he was supposed to be crazy."

"No. A doctor examined him," said Fenton Hardy. "He merely has a quirk in his mind, based on fear, about the Carabaya curse."

"Did he ever have red hair and use the name of Needles Ned?"

"No, only the name Blackbeard. He's not a crook, either. He had nothing to do with Bauer or the other counterfeiters. Of course, a guard will go along, so Señor Arezo will be safe. From what Blackbeard told us in regard to the cave, we believe he's telling the truth about the Doña Luisa coins."

It proved, several weeks later, that the self-styled pirate had indeed been telling the truth. The Arezo fortune was found where he had said it was, and the family was happy to have its name no longer connected with the unpleasant story of the *Curse of Carabaya*. Blackbeard went back to sea, a happy man.

"In the meantime," said Señor Arezo, smiling at Aunt Gertrude, "I believe you collect rare coins of women's heads, Miss Hardy. If you will be so kind as to accept this one which you have admired——"

He handed her the Doña Luisa piece.

"Oh, I can't take this. It's too valuable," objected Aunt Gertrude, greatly flustered.

"But you must. After all, it was the clue that restored my memory. It would be ungracious of me to take it away. Always," said Señor Arezo earnestly, "always I shall be most indebted to my dear friends, the Hardys."

While Aunt Gertrude was blushingly accepting the coin, Frank and Joe exchanged glances. Their minds held the same thoughts. They were glad, of course, that the puzzle regarding their unexpected visitor had been solved, and the mystery of the melted coins had been cleared up. Yet they felt a certain let-down feeling that nothing in the way of more detective work was brewing.

Mr Hardy guessed what his sons were thinking about. He smiled and said:

"It won't be long before you boys will be working on something new, I'll venture to say."

This was true. In a little while they were to find themselves involved in another mystery—*The Mystery of the Spiral Bridge.*

Just then the doorbell rang. Mr Hardy answered. Two policemen stood there with a prisoner.

"We have orders to see if Señor Arezo can identify this man," one of them said.

The Mexican readily recognized the suspect, who turned out to be another counterfeiter, as the person who had beaten and robbed him. Mr Hardy closed the door just as the telephone rang. He answered it, and found the caller to be Wu Sing.

"Have just heard coin thieves are safely in jail, so I shall receive no more threatening letters from them," he said. "Please to give your fine sons my congratulations. They warned me to guard Chinese coins. I appreciate pieces never reached melting pot."

Mr Hardy barely had time to deliver the message, when the telephone bell sounded again. Frank answered it this time.

"Listen," squeaked Chet's voice. "I've got big news!"

"So have we," Frank told him. "We found the counterfeiters who melted the coins, and——"

Chet interrupted him. "Tell me all about it tomorrow. But listen to *my* news. *I found the treasure!*"

"You're not fooling?"

"No sir-ee," shouted Chet. "The treasure of the Morton farm is ours. Remember the letter Dad found in the wall? Well, I read it again. Then I tried a new place a few feet away from the ditch. I hadn't dug more than five minutes before I hit the treasure."

"Good for you!" whooped Frank gleefully. "What was it? Coins?"

"Hundreds of 'em. And some old jewellery, too. And —and——"

"Yes?"

"Don't laugh. A book of recipes. My mother says she's going to use 'em and make some of the finest cakes for me——"

Frank was roaring with mirth.

"Hey, if you don't stop that, I shan't tell you the rest," complained the stout boy. "In the book was a letter. You fellows will be interested, because it tells about a mystery. I thought you'd want to solve it."

"Joe and I will be right over!" said Frank.